THE BORDER COUNTRY

THE BORDER COUNTRY

Lauran Paine

Chivers Press   •   Thorndike Press
Bath, England   Waterville, Maine USA

This Large Print edition is published by Chivers Press, England, and by Thorndike Press, USA.

Published in 2002 in the U.K. by arrangement with the author c/o Golden West Literary Agency.

Published in 2002 in the U.S. by arrangement with Golden West Literary Agency.

U.K. Hardcover ISBN 0–7540–4939–6 (Chivers Large Print)
U.K. Softcover   ISBN 0–7540–4940–X (Camden Large Print)
U.S. Softcover   ISBN 0–7862–4189–6 (Nightingale Series Edition)

The text of this Large Print edition is unabridged.
Other aspects of the book may vary from the original edition.

Set in 16 pt. New Times Roman.

Printed in Great Britain on acid-free paper.

British Library Cataloguing in Publication Data available

Library of Congress Cataloging-in-Publication Data
Paine, Lauran.
    The border country / by Lauran Paine.
       p. cm.
    ISBN 0–7862–4189–6 (lg. print : sc : alk. paper)
    1. Mexican American Border Region—Fiction. 2. Large type
    books. I. Title.
PS3566.A34 B66 2002
813'.54—dc21   2002020718

CHAPTER ONE

From the doorway of the Hardin house Dallas Benton watched Sheriff Tim Conley's posse cross out of the middle-morning distance, jaded horses swinging townward, slump-shouldered, slack-legged riders grey-powdered with the alkali dust of this border country, their rough faces burnt deepest brown, their flesh sag-muscled with strong weariness.

Tim Conley himself, ambling along slightly ahead, looked gaunt even from that distance and Dallas as well as everyone else who was watching the posse's return to Sunflower, knew Tim's dejection had more to do with failure than with the brassy sky and burning heat.

Summertime in the border country was a recurrent burden people had to live with. They accepted its terrible intensity unsmilingly, resigned or possibly fatalistically philosophical, but they bore it, and the bitter yellow sun made its daily crossing serenely indifferent to the azure-faded sky above or the suffering people down below.

Dallas followed the posse's progress as far as the livery-barn and there, as the men swung out and down to land heavily and stand close saying little, he could feel their bitterness, their dehydration, their raw-nerved tiredness all the

1

way across the roadway.

He moved down from Joel Hardin's porch, left the shade behind and slow-paced his way through that shimmering bright glare to stop finally where the posse was breaking up, some of its members going one way, some another way, but all pushing past the clutch of gathered townsmen without saying a single word to anyone.

Tim Conley alone remained, big legs wide-planted, sunken eyes bloodshot but thoroughly level, and slowly pushed out a great breath of air. He too ignored the people standing, expectantly waiting and fixed his gaze upon Dallas Benton where the latter halted, saying simply to this younger man, 'We didn't even get close to them.'

Dallas nodded; that much had been obvious from the attitude of Conley's possemen when they had returned to Sunflower. He watched the sheriff's dry eyes turn gratingly in their sockets saying nothing because there was nothing one could say to this announcement. A dozen men had tried their utmost and had failed; only the failure meant anything.

'How's Elizabeth?' Conley asked. 'I'd like to see her.'

Dallas led him back across the roadway, up onto Hardin's porch and into the house. Here, there was genuine coolness; not the usual border-country shade where a man stood in under a tree—when he could find one—and

2

was just as hot as out under the sun. Real, blessed coolness that touched down over every square inch of a hot man's hide.

Elizabeth Hardin lay with her eyes closed, her cheeks the identical colour as the alkali dust Conley was covered with, and her beautiful mouth loosely closed. Tim Conley bent his tall frame at the middle and forced a quiet smile over his red and heat-seared face.

'You sleeping, Elizabeth?' He asked very softly, and his familiar voice opened the lovely girl's eyes. His smile firmed up. 'Good girl. How do you feel?'

Elizabeth Hardin's greeny eyes seemed enormous against the pillow backgrounding her delicate features, pointing up more starkly than ever their symmetry, their unblemished flawlessness.

She did not answer the sheriff's question but said instead, 'You look worn out, Tim. You need a long rest.'

He drew away just a little, then affectionately, very gently lay a hand upon her shoulder. 'I am a little weary,' he conceded, then paused. 'But more'n that, Elizabeth, I'm disappointed.'

Her eyes kindled with understanding. 'Never mind,' she told him. 'Let them go. It's over with now and anyway why kill yourself or the others? It's done, Tim, and it's over.'

Dallas brushed fingers over the sheriff's arm with clear meaning. He jerked his head ever so

3

slightly at Tim Conley. His clear and youthful eyes were smokey with resolution, with demanding insistence.

Conley drew back his hand and solemnly winked down at the beautiful girl trying to make it as it had once been between them, a little gay, a little bantering. 'You take care,' he murmured to her. 'Hear now, Elizabeth? You take care and I'll be back directly.'

Back out in the parlour where drawn drapes made a cool gloominess Tim Conley faced Dallas Benton and raised his eyebrows.

'Not quite an even chance,' said Dallas in reply to that silently querying look. 'The bullet went in under her right arm, passed through her lungs and came out low on the left side.'

There was a red scar on Tim Conley's right hand; he considered it now turning the hand over and over as he continued to look downward saying nothing.

Dallas said: 'Where did you cross the line down into Mexico?'

'Below Borego Springs.'

'You trailed them that far?'

A nod.

'How many were there?'

'Ten. Maybe twelve.' Conley's eyes lifted. They were very grave. 'Americans,' he added. 'Americans, Dallas, not Mexicans.'

At this Dallas Benton's gaze turned hard, turned keen. 'You plumb sure, Sheriff?'

'Plumb sure. Mex renegades rarely ride

4

shod horses. Every one of those critters was fresh-shod. Mex outlaws scatter every which way after a raid, like Indians. Not these fellers. They went all together and they knew beforehand where they were going.'

'The Plummer gang, Sheriff?'

Tim Conley's big shoulders rose and fell. He sucked back a big breath of insufficient summer air; Dallas heard the long sweep of this wind go into him. Then he said, 'My guess is that it was the Plummer gang, Dallas. But that's just a guess. Jeb Plummer is in these parts; I know that to be true enough, boy.'

Conley considered the bleak-eyed tall youth before him. It took no great powers of divination to guess what was passing through the mind of Dallas Benton. Conley said, 'Don't try it.'

'Try what? What are you talking about?'

'Going down there after them alone.' Conley reached up to touch his raw-red neck where alkali particles worried the flesh like glass splinters. 'I know how you feel, Dallas, but it's no good that way, believe me.'

'I didn't say I was going to do that.'

'No,' agreed Conley, and added nothing to it, but was thinking privately that Dallas hadn't had to say anything; it had been written all over his face. 'I could tell you right now how it would end for you, if you did happen to try it.'

'Sheriff,' exploded the tall youth, his eyes rummaging Conley's face with their look of quiet desperation. 'Doc said her chances are getting poorer with every breath.'

'I know, Dallas, I know. But you gettin' killed isn't going to help her any.'

Past lips made ugly with anguish Dallas Benton said: 'I don't care for myself. I never in my life wanted another man dead as bad as I want *that man*.'

'Give me a couple of days to catch up here in town,' said Conley with his great patience. 'Then we'll make up another posse and go after them again.'

'Sure,' snapped the younger man. 'Sure, Sheriff. And what good'll come of it? U.S. lawmen have to stop at the border. Even the Army has to.'

'I'll wire ahead for permission to cross over.'

'You won't get it and you know you won't. If the Mex authorities would let you cross, the U.S. Army wouldn't.'

Tim Conley could not argue with this. International law forbade armed bodies of Americans crossing over into Mexico. Additionally, U.S. military authorities had never permitted a civilian posse to cross the line in pursuit of outlaws and it was hardly to be expected that they would in this case make any exception.

Sheriff Conley stood there trying to think of something to say to this angry young man, but he was ridden-down and weary to the very marrow of his bones and no thought would

6

come except the obvious one, and he knew without voicing it that if he prohibited Dallas Benton from going into Mexico after Elizabeth Hardin's assassin, he would simply be wasting his breath and his time.

'I'll see you later,' he murmured, passed over to the door and opened it, then lingered long enough to ask a final question.

'Where is Joel?'

'Probably at the stage station,' answered Dallas. 'He left here a little while ago.'

Conley gently eased the door closed; his hand dropped away from the latch heavily and for a moment he stood back in porch shade narrowing his glance against that outward glare and dancing heat. 'God damn it,' he said distinctly, then pushed out into the lemon-yellow brightness and went directly to the stage line office. There, he found Elizabeth's father exactly where Dallas had thought he might be: in his office.

Joel was mayor of Sunflower; he was also owner and operator of the local stage company, which was a feeder-line linked by back-country roads to the main arterial travelways. Joel was a short man of almost boyish build; he was at this time in his middle fifties.

He looked up from haggard eyes as Tim Conley entered the office. He had been sitting there in the gloom staring at nothing for nearly an hour and even Conley's appearance which

7

clearly was an intrusion upon his mood, did not at once alter nor entirely erase the look of desolation that showed layers deep in his eyes.

'You didn't find them,' said he grittily, turning his face away from the sheriff. 'I didn't expect that you would.'

This was the middle of another hot day; there was not a sound anywhere beyond the office and perhaps for that reason Joel Hardin's words went into Tim Conley leaving him rubbed a little raw. He crossed to a chair without comment and dropped down into it.

'They crossed over into Mexico below Borego Springs, Joel. We were maybe three hours behind them. Maybe a little less.'

'Yes,' said Elizabeth's father tartly. 'I knew it would be like that when you rode out.'

A slow rash of muddy colour flushed up into Sheriff Conley's face but he continued silent for a time; until the colour began to recede, then he said, 'Why isn't Doc with her? I just came over and only Dallas's with her. She needs expert care, Joel.'

'Don't tell me what she needs,' snapped Elizabeth's father. Then got control of himself, saying additionally, 'Doc went to get an old woman he knows out in the country; a midwife or something who is supposed to be a pretty fair all-around nurse. He said she's had lots of experience with gunshot wounds.'

Joel's tortured gaze turned slowly to stop upon Tim Conley's face. 'Did Dallas tell you

8

what Doc said?'

'Yes; he told me.'

'Tim; I'm offering five thousand dollars for the man who did that—dead and delivered to me here in Sunflower.' Joel paused, then added: 'Are you interested?'

Thoughts crowded together in Conley's mind: How could you offer a reward for a man you didn't know, had never seen, and no one else except a dying girl had seen? And why should he, Tim Conley, be any more interested now than he'd been before; Elizabeth had come to him often as a little girl in pigtails for help in tying her first hackamore-knot. She had also come to him later when womanhood's full bloom was upon her, and he'd tried his level best to answer the questions she'd asked him then, too.

He said to Joel: 'You have a lot of guts to say a thing like that to me. Damn you; I've whipped the stuffin' out of men a lot better than you are, Joel Hardin, for sayin' a lot less to me.'

He arose to stand sturdily in the little office looking stonily at the smaller man behind the desk.

'I wouldn't touch your lousy five thousand dollars with a forty-foot pole. I want that man as badly as you do. But not for money—for Elizabeth. And for all the other Elizabeths he'll shoot sooner or later if he's left to run free.'

Conley stood there waiting, breathing deeply, but Elizabeth's father said nothing. He did not even look up. So Conley said the rest of what was on his mind.

'You publicise an offer like that and you'll attract every bounty hunter in Texas. You don't know how they work, Joel, but I do. There'll appear here in town three or four of them one day, and every one of 'em'll have a corpse tied over his saddle. And every one of them will swear to high heaven that *his* dead man is the feller who shot Elizabeth.

'But not a one of them will be the right man. They'll be instead just some luckless devils who were riding along minding their own business who got shot from ambush for your lousy five thousand dollars.'

Still Joel did not speak nor raise his eyes, nor even move in his chair.

Conley said, 'I've got to get some fresh air,' and stalked out of the office, paused upon Sunflower's broad board walkway long enough to look north and south out of long habit, then went along as far as his jailhouse, and there at last found surcease from both his weariness and his troubles, for this building, one of the few remaining adobe structures in Sunflower, had walls three feet thick. No amount of fierce sun-smash ever disturbed the serenity or the coolness within.

He was standing alone, he thought, letting this coolness winnow the anger from his system, when a female voice spoke out of the shadows far back, saying with strong bitterness: 'This lousy country.'

Conley spun around on the balls of his feet every raw nerve-end alive to a second presence where he had thought there was none.

The girl sauntered forward. She was all woman; Conley noticed that in one swiftly masculine glance. She approached him with a kind of challenging grace; her eyes were the true colour of midnight. She stopped close and looked steadily forward. The heat did not seem to touch her and in the pleasant non-glare of Conley's jailhouse she stood strong-backed and motionless.

Her eyes had a direct watchfulness and her expression now wore an expressionless, set calm. It was, Conley thought, a look of deep fatalism, if it was any kind of an expression at all. She was the kind of a woman whose presence struck down into a man, and perhaps years later in the watch-hours of the night a man would recall her vividly as she now was.

Conley was, for all his tiredness, acutely conscious of her there in the office with him. He said: 'Who are you?'

'Rose Bell,' answered the girl, studying Conley's red-raw and rugged face.

'What were you doing in here?'

'Waiting for you.'

'Why?'

Rose Bell's expressionless gaze began to

11

brighten with hard irony, but only for a second, then her gravity, her very definite pride, settled again and there was nothing to be read from her features at all.

'I want to help you catch the man who shot that girl,' Rose Bell said.

Conley considered this, then asked: 'Do you think you can?'

Rose Bell's shoulders moved. 'Perhaps,' she murmured. 'I arrived in Sunflower yesterday. About the time those outlaws found that girl after the stage robbery and shot her. I came here from Nacori. Do you know where that is?'

'Over the line in Mexico,' said Conley evenly, watching this girl, weighing and evaluating her.

'There are many kinds of men in Nacori, Sheriff.'

Conley inclined his head; he knew the village of Nacori although he had had no reason to go down there these past few years.

'I worked in a *cantina* down there. I saw many outlaws come and go.'

Conley let his body turn loose and easy-standing. He motioned towards a chair meaning for Rose Bell to sit down. She remained standing.

'Do you know the Plummer gang, Sheriff?'

'I know who they are, yes.'

'Murderers and bandits and worse,' said Rose Bell fiercely. 'Stage robbers. I heard them speaking of coming up here to waylay a stage, Sheriff.'

'They waylaid it,' said Conley dryly. 'They got a six thousand dollar haul. It was afterwards that they came on Elizabeth Hardin out riding and shot her. Left her for dead.'

'So she couldn't identify them,' said the handsome girl with the same bitterness in her tone.

'Probably that was it,' concurred the lawman. Then he said, 'But there's no proof either way. I'm sure in my heart it was Jeb Plummer's outfit but you can't use that kind of evidence in a court of law.'

Rose Bell appeared to be thoughtfully turning something over in her mind. Finally she said, 'This Elizabeth Hardin—can I see her?'

Conley straightened up. 'I suppose so,' he said. 'I'll take you to her.' But he made no immediate move doorward, instead he continued to assess Rose Bell, and eventually he said, 'She's pretty sick.'

'Most shot people get that way, Sheriff.'

'Yeah.'

Still Conley stood there. He was plumbing the depths of his mind for a solution to the problem Rose Bell presented: How, exactly, could she help him? She could not go to Nacori with him; no one excepting the injured girl had seen the men . . .

That was it! Elizabeth could describe the gunman and Rose Bell could identify him from that.

'Come on,' he said, wheeling doorward. 'Only we can't stay long.'

Rose Bell gave Conley's back a peculiar look but said nothing as she followed him out into the angry brightness.

CHAPTER TWO

Unkempt Doctor Albigence Semple was there in the room when Sheriff Conley and Rose Bell entered. He cast them a jaundiced look from the bedside, his disillusioned eyes lingering longest upon the girl, then he moved away making room.

Tim crossed over to stop and peer down. Elizabeth's gaze raised, warmed, and she smiled. For that moment she was pretty and pleased and very young looking again; then she saw Rose Bell standing there considering her gravely from an expressionless face, and her smile faded.

'Is this the nurse?' She asked in her faint, tired-sounding voice.

Doctor Semple's glance flung around to halt upon Rose Bell, but he said nothing.

Tim would have answered, but now Rose Bell drew forth something from the top of her dress and bent a little, saying, 'Do you recognise any of these men?'

She was holding a recent photograph close to the wounded girl's face. Tim Conley bent quickly to see this picture; there was a flicker of hope firming up in his face.

Elizabeth's forehead faintly crinkled; her eyes drew out narrow in concentration, then she lay back looking over the photo's rim at Rose Bell. 'That man standing behind the other man's chair with his hand upon the seated man's shoulder.'

'Yes?' urged Conley. 'Do you recognise him?'

'He's the one who shot me.'

Doctor Semple, watching from across the room, saw Conley draw gradually upright; heard his breath pass out in a gentle sigh. He saw the girl return the picture to its place in her bodice, and he moved up to stand across Elizabeth's bed. 'I need you,' he now told this strange girl. 'Elizabeth's got to have twenty-four hour attention. There is no one else I can get. Will you nurse her?'

Tim, gazing with almost disinterest upon the medical man, said now, 'Joel told me you went after some woman out in the country.'

'She's down in bed with the grippe,' said Semple shortly, returning his attention at once to Rose Bell. 'You name your price, girl. I'll guarantee it.'

Rose Bell did not answer right away; she was watching how Elizabeth Hardin gazed up at Sheriff Conley. She also saw how his hand

15

gently pushed back the injured girl's hair from her face. She was thinking that this big sun-blackened man with his holstered gun and sweat-darkened shell-belt, had a way with women. His hand was so gentle there upon the pillow, so kind and reassuring. She answered Doctor Semple through a rising blur, pushing out the words in her own way.

'Of course I'll stay with her; but I've no knowledge of nursing—except for knife wounds and broken bones, and not much of that.'

Semple's disillusioned eyes warmed towards Rose Bell, and at her side she could feel without seeing it, that distinct expression of strong approval Tim Conley turned on her. This latter, for some reason, made her look down at Elizabeth, for although she was not a reticent or retiring person naturally, Conley's approval far more than Doctor Semple's, left her not quite sure of herself, and inwardly vastly more unnerved than she would have admitted to even herself. Elizabeth smiled upwards into Rose Bell's eyes.

Doctor Semple turned away again, going as far as a little table where his black bag lay, and there busied himself with several small bottles. Sheriff Conley touched Rose Bell saying softly, 'See me to the door, will you, Miss Bell?'

They passed back through the cool rooms and just short of the front doorway Conley turned, facing fully around, his voice different than it had been in the sick-room. 'Let me see

16

that picture,' he said in an unmistakable tone. Then, when Rose Bell dutifully handed it forward, he took it, asking: 'Is this Jeb Plummer's gang?'

'Yes.'

'Where did you get hold of this?'

'Down in Nacori—where else?'

Conley looked across at her. 'Can you name these men for me?'

'Yes. I'll write each name on the back of the picture and have it for you when you come back.'

Conley pushed out his hand and after Rose Bell took back the photograph, he studied her over an interval of long silence.

'Will you tell me—why? Why are you doing this?'

The girl's direct gaze did not drop away when she answered. 'Do you want a pound of flesh too? I came here; I agreed to help you; I will nurse that girl in there. Do I have to give you my soul too?'

Conley, facing this girl's inexpressive calm; her compelling handsomeness and her utter honesty, felt that behind her was some kind of a mystery. He lowered his gaze, altered his voice, and said, 'No. I'm sorry,' and reached behind him for the door latch. He was searching for other words as he opened the door, and eventually found them.

'I don't mean to sound ungrateful. You see, I watched that girl in there grow up. When her

17

paw'd go out of town years back I'd sort of mother-and-father her.' He brought down his steady gaze and it softened towards Rose Bell. 'I'll come back after supper, ma'am.'

He then left the Hardin house. Closed the door gently and had no knowledge that behind it Rose Bell still stood there quietly recalling and assessing his words and his features.

He had progressed along the southerly roadway only part way to his office when Doc Semple's hurrying footfalls and voice halted him. He turned, waiting.

'One damnfool thing after t'other,' groaned the medical man, coming up and turning his caustic face towards the sheriff. 'What you goin' to do about that young hothead?'

'What young hothead are you talking about, Doc?'

'Why; young Benton, of course.'

With something solid beginning to form behind his belt-buckle, Sheriff Conley asked what Dallas had done.

'He loaded his guns, took his horse from the livery-barn, two canteens full o' water—and went south,' answered Semple. 'An' you know blessed well why he did it and what he's up to. Now then . . .'

'Slow down, Doc. Just slow down. How long ago did he ride out?'

'Maybe an hour. Maybe an hour and a half.'

Conley squared fully around to gaze into Doctor Semple's face. He was unsmiling.

'Doc,' he asked with deceptive mildness, 'did you know about this when I was up at Joel's place?'

'Certainly. He left before that.'

Conley began to gently nod his head. 'I'm going to let you in on a little secret,' he said. 'An hour's start south towards Mexico is about the same as a day's start—or a week's start—or a month's start. You can't push a horse in this heat, Doc. Not across the desert. So a man who starts out an hour ahead of you, is just that far ahead all the way to the line—and over it.'

Semple scowled as he coloured. He knew he was being considered a fool. 'I'm a doctor, not a saddle-horse-man,' he grumbled. 'How would I know about things like that?'

'By listening,' explained the sheriff dryly. 'Just by listenin' when folks talk.' He continued to regard Semple from guileless eyes. 'Doc; I hope you're a better medicine man than you are a frontiersman.'

Sheriff Conley left to walk sturdily across to the liverybarn. There, he ascertained that Dallas had indeed ridden out—but it had been more like two and a half hours earlier, than one and a half hours.

He went next to his jailhouse, and there, in the utter peacefulness with languid, cool air sweeping over him, he considered the old iron army cot in his solitary strap-steel cell. No bed he had seen in his entire lifetime had ever

19

looked so inviting. He crossed over to pass beyond the open door and ease down. He balanced there for only a moment, then dumped his hat carelessly upon the floor, swung up his legs and lay back with his body turning gradually loose all over, softening against the ticking until he groaned.

He could not have slept more than two hours, and it seemed more like two minutes, when someone's insistent plucking awakened him. He stirred, fought up from beneath wave after wave of total bliss and blackness, and recognised Albigence Semple's voice even before the rawboned, unappealing face cleared into focus before his eyes.

'All right. All right, Doc. This is the only shirt I own that isn't patched so don't tear it off me. What's the trouble now?'

'Joel's coming down here. Go wash your face. Don't be loafing when he gets here, for heaven's sake.'

Conley pushed himself half up and teetered on the bunk's raw edge caustically regarding the doctor. 'Didn't Joel ever hear of a plumb tuckered out man before?'

'He's in no mood fo—'

'Doc,' interrupted Conley, his voice acquiring an edge as he arose, brushed a big hand through his shock-headed mane and headed past towards a wash basin and water pitcher, 'Doc, I don't care what Joel Hardin thinks. I've been thirty-six hours on the trail

20

without sleep.' Conley filled the basin, splashed water into his face and spoke through it. 'Joel can go to hell. I'm only a man, Doc. Just flesh and blood and bone. I've done the best I could do up to now. I'm plumb satisfied no one around here could have done any better including Joel . . . where's that cussed towel?'

'Here.'

'Thanks.'

There came now the sharply solid footfalls of someone of no very great weight entering the office. Conley lowered the towel just enough to see over its edge. Joel Hardin stood before him, lips tight-drawn, eyes unnaturally alight. Conley did not give Elizabeth's father a chance to speak.

'You turn right around and walk back out of here,' he ordered. 'Go on now, Joel—get!'

The towel came all the way down as Hardin made no move to obey. Conley's utterly still face and bloodshot eyes meant business.

'I swear to you, Joel, if you're still standing there one minute from now I'll heave you out into the roadway. You and Doc both.'

Joel fell back as far as the door. From there he said, 'Are you going after Dallas?'

Conley watched Semple move past and stop just beyond Hardin. 'Yes,' he said, 'I'm going after the simpleton. And maybe when I get my hands on him I'll take his shellbelt and blister his hide with it, too, because it goes against my grain to be shot at over a young damned fool like him.'

'You better make up another posse,' said Hardin.

Conley tossed aside the towel, fetched his hat and crushed it down upon his head saying, 'Joel; folks say you're a pretty good stage-line manager. Do you reckon that's so?'

Hardin's eyes narrowed. He said nothing.

'Because if it is so,' continued the sheriff, 'then maybe you'd better stick to running your business and letting me run mine. I don't want a damned posse—can you get that through your thick skull.'

'What can one man do?'

'Sometimes one man's a lot better than an army. Particularly if he's going where an army can't go.'

Doctor Semple drew in his breath sharply. With widening eyes he said, 'Tim; they'll kill you. You saw how many of them there were in that picture. Besides, Nacori's a death-trap for U.S. lawmen.'

Joel Hardin shot a quick look at the medical man. 'Nacori? Doc; do you and Tim know something I should know?'

'The only thing you should know,' cut in Sheriff Conley, 'is that Doc's tongue has a hinge in the middle and wags at both ends. Now I'm telling you two for the last time—scat!'

Doctor Semple moved back a discreet little distance but Joel stood his ground. 'When are

22

you leaving?' He demanded of the lawman.

'Not until dark. Do you want to know why not until then? I'll tell you: Because the night is the best time to try and cover a lot of ground in the desert in the summertime. I can't make the crossing in one day or one night, so I make as good time as I can tonight. That satisfy you, Joel?'

'It satisfies me, Tim,' replied Hardin in a quiet tone. 'Tim . . .?'

'What?'

'I'd like to apologise for this afternoon. You'll know how I felt when you came in.'

Sheriff Conley stood briefly silent, then he nodded saying in an altered voice, 'Sure, Joel. I'd have acted the same way. Forget it.'

'Good luck, Tim.'

'Thanks. Joel . . .?'

'Yes?'

'I'll be easy on Dallas. You watch over my foster-daughter for me.'

Hardin and Doctor Semple walked northerly from the jailhouse. Tim Conley listened to their fading footfalls for a moment longer, then he too went out into the diminishing day.

Once, when Tim Conley had been a young man, his father had said to him: 'Son; sometime in every man's life he wants so badly to kill someone he could bury his hands to the wrists in their guts. When that day comes for you remember this: You might be the man someone hates that much. You surely will be if you kill out of pure hatred because that's one thing that can't be hidden—murder. And even if your victim has no kin or friends to avenge him, he will have his revenge for as long as you live to draw breath. His revenge will be your conscience.'

Conley thought of those words now. He tried to balance them against the compelling urge he'd had burning in his heart for several sleepless days now—the urge to kill a man and stand over his last agonies smiling.

He moved away from his jailhouse still remembering those words.

Tim Conley had been a peace officer for eighteen years; in all that time he'd never before actually wished he might kill another man. Now he did.

CHAPTER THREE

A variety of coolness came, with the lowering red sun falling away and shadows forming in the late afternoon, but it would be several hours yet before the heat dissipated, and until then Sheriff Conley had several things to do.

He bought a bath at the barber shop, and he afterwards donned fresh clothing at the jailhouse, shaved himself and combed his hair, then he went across to the cafe and ate enough for two ordinary men, passed out into the dying day and there made a cigarette and smoked it.

Around him Sunflower was relaxing; turning away from its every-day pursuits and standing hushed in the coming dusk, scenting the peculiarly acrid fragrance of cooling earth and curing grass and dying day.

For this peaceful little while there would be no one abroad; in four dozen homes people would be having supper. For this moment even Sunflower's two saloons, *The Texican* and *The Jeff Davis House*, would have empty hitchrails.

Tim Conley stood smoking, considering his town, thinking that the people were decent folk, tough and self-reliant. But always in the van of his thoughts was the knowledge of what he must do. He looked far out where the sun was redly sliding away, knowing in his heart a kind of futility. He had to do this thing but he had seldom ever wanted to do something less.

He finished the cigarette and started along for Joel Hardin's place. There remained but one more thing to be seen to, then he'd head south.

Joel himself answered Conley's gentle knocking. He stood there emanating a kind of awkward comradeship, waiting for the sheriff to speak.

'How is she, Joel?'

'No change,' stated Elizabeth's parent.

'I'd like to see Rose Bell if I could, Joel.'

'Sure,' said Hardin, and turned without another word to pass back into the hushed house leaving Tim Conley standing in the doorway.

A little time passed then Rose Bell appeared, her reaching glance touching Conley before she stopped in the doorway, brought forth a hand and offered the photograph. 'The names are on the back,' she stated.

He took the picture, considered it in brief silence, then pocketed it saying, 'Would you take a little walk with me?'

She moved out onto the porch closing the door behind them, and passed out of Joel Hardin's yard with Conley. Around them dusk was puddling and although the sun was totally gone now there yet lingered that long last paleness in the west which precluded full dark. They went north, as far as the walkway lasted, then walked slowly farther out.

'How is she?' Conley asked, referring to the girl in both their thoughts.

'Doctor Semple is with her. There doesn't appear to be any change.' She looked sideways at his profile; at the strong thrust of jaw and the wide forehead. 'It was such a pointless thing to do, shooting her like that.'

'To keep their identity a secret,' he murmured.

She snorted. 'People would have guessed.'

'The law requires positive identification.'

'This rotten country,' she said, repeating the

first remark she had ever made to him. 'What law? Plummer's gang will never be tried in a court. You know that, Sheriff.'

They circled a shaggy paloverde tree treading its fallen golden blossoms, and stopped there while he worked up a cigarette with his face averted.

She stood motionless watching him. 'It's killing that boy.'

He lit up and exhaled turning to gaze down into her face. 'He may be expediting that, riding off alone like he did. There's no protection for his kind over the line in Mexico, and he's too hot-headed to step lightly.'

'You wouldn't have done as much?'

He gave her a slow, smiling look. 'Probably I'd have done the same thing, ma'm, at his age.'

'You're not so much older.'

His eyes continued to twinkle at her. 'Enough older,' he murmured, 'to know that dead heroes are a dime a dozen.'

She watched his face with her calm and judging look. 'You are a man who talks one way and feels another way. You would do exactly as Dallas Benton has done.' She hesitated, selecting her next words with great care. 'But you would not be killed down there. You are one of those men who was born middle-aged.'

'What kind of a man is that, ma'm?'

'A wise man, Sheriff. The kind of a man who

sees things without trying to see them; who feels things without knowing how he feels them. The kind of a man who makes a good friend, and a deadly enemy.'

'You must have made quite a study of men,' he said to her, without any trace of irony in his voice.

'I've had to. Men carry the vision of their ideal woman in their minds. Every woman they meet they try to mould to fit that likeness. And afterwards, because no woman can be all things to a man, they leave her and go on to the next woman. For the man this is like shedding his skin. For the woman it can be a lot different; it can be hell on earth. It can be shame and anguish and bitter, bitter memories.' She put forth a hand to touch the paloverde's green trunk. She was no longer looking at Conley, but was staring far out.

His cigarette lay forgotten between two fingers. He said gently, 'Rose; it works both ways. Women expect too much. A man is as he is, and he does what he must do, and it seldom is the right thing or the romantic thing, or maybe even the respectable thing.'

Now she gazed at him. Her features were shadowed and strangely sweet in the dusk; she seemed a girl again; a very sturdy and handsome girl of the border country.

'You're right of course, Sheriff. Probably a woman, like a man, has a picture built up that actually is not one man or one woman—but many men and many women.'

He nodded, re-lighting the cigarette and taking back a great inhalation. She heard the sweep of smoke go into him. Then it came out faintly, muffling his next words.

'A country is the same way. You see here what you want to see. If you have some idea of waterfalls and great pine forests—then the desert is bleak and ugly to you. But I've never seen a country I would call an ideal place. Where the forests and waterfalls are, Rose, there is usually two feet of snow for six months out of the year and cold so bad it hurts to breathe it. You said this was a rotten country.' He paused to drop the cigarette and grind it out. 'It's not the country that is bad. A country, itself, cannot be bad. It's the people and the way of life that make a land bad.' He looked out over the faint lift and fall of country northward. Then he deliberately turned and gazed southward. When next he spoke it was on a quite different topic; one which was now, and had been for some time, uppermost in his thoughts.

'Which one was it, Rose?'

She considered him steadily through a long moment of stillness, and although she readily enough surmised what he was wondering, she asked the obvious question nevertheless. 'Which one—what, Sheriff?'

His gaze left off studying the southward flow of country, and fell evenly to her face.

'Which one of the men in the picture was it that tried to mould you?'

'It is not important. Not now. That was another girl and another lifetime.'

She twisted slightly from the waist so that only her profile remained within his sight. But even head-on he could have read nothing anyway, because that look of inexpressive calm had settled upon her face again. Still, even this, unreadable though it was to him, was not altogether without meaning. It was, he now thought, a kind of mask she used to hide hurt, or recollection, or anything she wished for the world not to see.

'Do you hope this man gets killed?' he asked her.

'I don't know. I've never wanted anyone hurt before.' She was for a time still and silent, then she said, 'I am tough, Sheriff. I've had to be. So it's not for me; at least I tell myself that. I say it's for the girls like Elizabeth Hardin that I want him punished. Sheriff . . .?'

'Yes.'

'He is thoroughly evil. He is bad all the way through. It was like awakening from a bad dream when I finally saw him as he is. I was sick and degraded and terribly ashamed.'

'So you ran away. Came up here to Sunflower.'

'Yes.'

She turned fully away from him now. He saw her shoulders lift suddenly and jerk, then

30

settle again. She was silently crying.

He stood there regarding her; from their first meeting his interest in her had been direct and lively, and right now his vision of her was very distinct. She was tall and abundantly shapely in a way that struck down into a man— a good man or a bad man. Her composed face held back some kind of deep knowledge; her brave eyes mirrored womankind's ancient wisdom too.

Never before had a woman compelled his attention, its deepest interest, as this woman did. He thought of the way she held her head when she looked at a person, still and straight, and he thought of her long silences too.

These latter left him unsure. Silence in a woman like Rose Bell meant many things, and in reflection now, this knowledge played uncertainly upon his thinking, lifting in him a slow run of excitement as though he were on the edge of some discovery.

Then she was turning back and speaking again, scattering his thoughts with that faint though persevering irony of her tone.

'You got it out of me didn't you? That's all you wanted.'

'Not all,' said Conley slowly. 'And I had a reason.'

'Curiosity. A man's curiosity about a woman.'

'No,' he told her, unoffended by the sharpness of her look, of her tone. 'I'm not a curious man. Obey the law in Sunflower, don't be troublesome, and I don't care what a man or a woman has been. Life is a pretty complicated matter, Rose Bell. I don't suppose there's a mature person alive who hasn't gotten a little dirt on them sometime. I don't look for that in folks; I judge people by their actions.' Conley rubbed his jaw. 'If you come right down to it, I'm not qualified to judge anyway, but every person weighs other people. I think the best way to do this is by watching folks; see how they behave. I've lived long enough to realise that intentions and words aren't worth much—only actions really mean anything.'

'Then why did you want to know?'

'Well,' began Conley, taking his time with this reply, feeling for the words carefully. 'After I take you home tonight I'm heading south after Dallas Benton.'

'Only after him, Sheriff?'

'No; after the man Elizabeth identified in your picture too. I reckon I'll find them all right. Particularly the man in the picture. I aim to keep on searching until I do.'

'And . . . ?'

'Well, Rose Bell, I don't want to cause you more hurt, and if that man is the one you loved it would make a difference.'

'No difference,' she said huskily. 'I don't think you can take him alive. But if you could you'd only be prolonging something because no court in Texas would keep him from a gallows.'

That, thought Conley, was the gospel truth; Texas courts considered no extenuating circumstances. When a man shot a woman his time on earth was afterwards limited to the length of time he could keep clear of the law.

But Conley was also thinking of something else. If Elizabeth's assassin were legally hanged there would be nothing to stand between him and Rose Bell, but if he killed this man, there would be. No amount of explaining-away ever mitigated a thing like that, Conley knew.

Rose Bell studied Conley's face for a long time before speaking, then she started away from the paloverde tree saying only, 'It's late; I think we'd better be getting back.'

They returned leisurely the way they had come with full night down around them, its shielding darkness full of coolness, fragrance and eternal promise. At the Hardins' front walk Rose Bell turned with swift resolve to say, 'In a man's world, Sheriff, a woman's words carry very little weight. But I think you should heed it when I warn you. Down in Nacori there are no honest men; there are some less vicious than others, but there's not a man who wouldn't kill for money. They will kill a stranger rather than ask questions. You must be very, very careful.'

'They know me in Nacori?' Conley said.

Rose Bell nodded, seeing him stalwart in the shadows; seeing him unsmiling and loose-standing with his thoughtful gaze fixed strongly upon her. 'I suppose they do,' she murmured. 'You're the kind of a man other men remember. Well . . . good luck, Sheriff.'

'Tim,' he told her. 'Just plain Tim.'

'Tim . . .'

She raised up suddenly to lean against him and feel for his lips in the night; to kiss him with a passion which was equal parts hunger and sorrow. Then she dropped back down, spun away and fled up the walk to the house beyond.

Conley went along slowly to where he kept his animal. He saddled it mechanically, his thoughts distant and his expression troubled. She had not told him whether the man in the picture was the one she'd fled from, and remembering now each lift of eyes, each changing expression, he could not make up his mind whether this was the man or not.

He finally slapped down the stirrup-leather, turned to bridle his horse, and pushed these thoughts away from him. It shouldn't really matter anyway, for as she'd intimated, whoever he was, he was living on borrowed time anyway.

Those folks who said there was good in the worst men of this world deluded themselves, he thought, standing for a moment in the shed doorway gazing out over a land gone silent, gone still and empty. Where was there good in a man who would ride up to a young girl out riding for pleasure, draw his gun and deliberately shoot her out of the saddle and sit there for a moment watching her agony, her flowing blood?

He faced back around reaching for the reins.

CHAPTER FOUR

Conley rode down the night southerly with a strong creosote-bush scent preceding him into the desert. He struck and crossed a dry creek bed, then, where the scrub thickened, let his horse pick its way around cat-claw, paloverde, and the endless varieties of cacti.

Near midnight he cut the Borego Springs trace, which was no more actually than a sifted-over vague trail kept packed by the wildlife that inhabited this scorched and ragged, long sweep of land, and there, for the first and last time, he booted his animal over into a rolling lope that covered mile after mile.

Beyond midnight he drank deeply from his canteen, screwed the cap firmly down and did not touch the water again until near dawn.

Farther south, the land became broken and rutted. There were erosion gullies running like aged wrinkles in every direction. Starshine helped Conley's mount make his way; he was a sagacious beast, and Conley had selected him for this virtue rather than for speed. He couldn't, as Conley had often stated, run fast enough to catch a cold; but his wise and conserving canniness, coupled to a toughness that made him appear never to tire, had also inspired Conley to say often, that if whoever he was trailing did not take to the air, this horse would eventually overtake him. And it was true; had been proved true many times.

With new light appearing softly to the east, Conley began searching for a good place to hole-up and wait-out this long-burning day ahead, for short of relaying mounts, it was impossible regardless of how much 'bottom' a saddle animal possessed, to reach Borego Springs the first day out.

This, too, was the first test of a man and his horse in desert country. If he could find shade and remain there totally unmoving, he would not need so much water and he might be able to live long enough to reach the Springs by the following dawn. If not, he died. It was as simple as that, for neither man nor animal could endure, in this heat-tortured country, more than eight hours without water—unless they knew the tricks of survival.

Conley knew them; he had made this crossing many times, so while the first faint flush of pink dawn came to soften this deadly world he was passing over, he sought and found, what he needed most.

It was a narrow gulch, deeper than most, cut by the fierce and torrential winter floods that scourged this sorry country. He dismounted to consider it with an experienced eye. It was narrow, which meant that when the sun finally struck down into it, then passed beyond, Conley would be under those dehydrating rays for perhaps something like one hour. It was also deep enough for his horse to find a modicum of shelter too. And finally, along the crumbling sidewalls there grew occasional tufts of forage grass, each plant clinging with the stubborn determination of most desert verdure, to the cracked earth.

Conley made a cigarette and smoked it while standing upon the brink of this gulley. He off-saddled and, with the promising sun beginning to pour its molten gold down over the land while it was still hidden from sight, he led the horse down into his gully. There came to both of them almost at once a lingering of the night's pleasant, shadowy coolness. Conley bent to hobble the horse, remove its split-ear bridle, then step back so the beast could hop past, which it did by sucking back upon its haunches, then springing forward. To this animal, obviously, hobbles were nothing new.

Beyond that, for Conley, there was nothing much to do but settle against the stony soil and wait. Lying full length, one arm propped against his head, Conley listened to his thoughts, the only interruption an occasional shifting of his horse farther along the ravine, and the crunch of its teeth when something edible turned up.

The ground beneath him was still cool although, by now, the sun was riding well above the horizon; hanging there huge and bitterly dazzling. Not a breath of air stirred and the overhead sky was turning its customary summer-burnished pale, pale blue.

He had found no horse-tracks en route to this spot, but then he'd only indifferently watched for them in the night, because, knowing how Dallas Benton would think, he scarcely expected the younger man to travel towards the border in a line others might follow.

He would find them, though, at Borego Springs. He was confident of that. Borego Springs was the only year-round watering site in this entire southerly sweep of country. There were always fresh tracks there, and this, more than anything else, had provided Conley with the knowledge he'd needed for his earlier pursuit of the outlaws who had robbed the stage north of Sunflower, and shot Elizabeth Hardin. Borego Springs was the lodestar which drew all desert travellers, good or bad.

Morning waned into afternoon and for a time the sun's direct rays burnt with terrible intensity down into Conley's ravine. This lasted a little more than an hour, as he'd speculated it would, then the sun passed overhead and Conley took his first drink. He afterwards, with cooling sweat running under his shirt, hid his face beneath his hat and slept.

With the afternoon well along he awakened, rinsed his mouth, spat, and sat up to smoke a cigarette. He had badly needed that rest. Sweat rolled across his forehead to a juncture above his nose, then ran downward to drip against the ground. He wiped a shirt-sleeve over his face, took a final inhalation off the cigarette and killed it.

How long, he now asked himself solemnly, does a man's patience last? The Plummer gang had been operating out of Nacori, south of the border, for almost a year now. Its members had robbed and rustled and thus far no one had ever apprehended even one member of the gang. Two U.S. marshals, the sheriff of the adjoining county, and a grim band of Texas Rangers, at one time or another had all sought Plummer and his comrades, who had eluded every attempt at capture and ambush, to pass swiftly down into Mexico after their raids, and laughingly send up word that lawmen were fools and worse.

Conley had thought before, and he mused in this same vein now, that where legal barriers, international laws and large posses of armed men had failed; it was quite possible one man might succeed. He had considered this, yes, but, as he'd told Rose Bell, he himself was a prudent man.

Then what, his inner voice asked, was he doing down here now? This was not the act of a prudent man; it wasn't even the act of a very smart man, because canny Jeb Plummer with his fierce black beard and cunning eyes, would have spies along the border who would see every passing stranger and report their arrival to the bandit chief.

Well, he said back to himself, there *is* a limit to patience. When the Plummers start shooting down young girls it's different than simply stealing bullion off stages, and since a man has to face his conscience each morning when he looks in the mirror to shave, he knows full well what must be done, and he then rides out to do it.

As for Dallas Benton, that was a bird of a different feather. Dallas was a hot-head; he'd always been one, and Conley had known him as long as he'd known Elizabeth. He loved Elizabeth though, and in Conley's eyes this made a difference—more of a difference actually than Conley would have admitted to himself. But, he told himself now, getting up stiffly and squinting along the ravine for his horse, he would not have embarked upon this trail he was riding just for young Dallas Benton. He sighted the horse standing hip-shot, lower lip hanging, half asleep, and moved towards it bridle in hand. Or would he have? Well; it was pointless to consider this, because

40

he was on his way to succour Dallas Benton as a sort of side-issue, so perhaps it amounted to the same thing.

He saddled up, climbed up out of the arroyo and stood upon its upper shoulder with the horse at hand, turning his head back and forth seeking—he knew not what.

Afterwards, with an hour or so left of daylight, he resumed his way southward. Riding along through a silence that crowded up around him endlessly, he thought of Jeb Plummer.

There was not a lot known about Plummer. He had been a guerrilla during the war. It was said, like other guerrillas, when the fighting ended and others returned to former homes and former ways, Jeb Plummer had found this impossible. It was known that he'd raided in Kansas and Missouri before turning southerly into Texas. It was also known for a fact that he was a madman in battle; enough lawmen had survived brushes with his gang to testify to this. But beyond these things—and his description—there was only rumour to go by, and Conley knew that Texas rumours were apt to be the most elaborately embroidered lies under the sun. Texans had that knack.

Jeb Plummer stood six feet tall. He wore a full facebeard that was black and curly. Plummer was known to be very vain about this beard. He was a centaur when mounted and was a deadly man with a gun—in either hand.

He smiled often and was lavish with his money—as he could well afford to be since his boldness kept him well provided with it. He was vicious and cruel and as deadly as a sidewinder, but he was also a canny man; he handed out gold with a smile and a gallant flourish among the border Mexicans, and they being an impressionable and romantically-minded people, blessed him for a heroic bandit *jefe*; a man of historic proportions. They were inalienably his friends.

Conley knew all this firsthand. He rode along through lowering shadows considering it, and some time before nightfall fully fell, he told himself wryly that if he succeeded in what he had in mind it would be the miracle of all border country miracles.

Two things in particular bothered him. The first one was simply that, although he too had friends around Nacori, respectable Mexicans of substance and honour, he did not think it would be wise to seek them out. At least for a while it would be better if no one knew he was in the area.

His second problem was more difficult; he especially wanted one man, whose name was Burl Cassady. It had been this man whom Elizabeth had identified, and whom Rose Bell had named for him. He did not want to arouse Plummer's entire gang against him if this could be avoided. What he specifically wished to do was locate Cassady, waylay him, then race back

42

to Sunflower with Cassady as his prisoner.

It would be simpler of course simply to kill Burl Cassady, but Sheriff Tim Conley wanted Cassady to suffer; a bullet was swift and too final for a man like Cassady who arbitrarily shot down young women. Conley wanted him to sweat and groan and pant. He was perfectly willing to risk his own life to accomplish this.

As he at long last hove into sight of Borego Springs where pewter starshine shone softly against the little, still pool of springwater, he thought that, doubtful as his plan seemed, it was far from impossible—until one reflected that somewhere on ahead rode fiery Dallas Benton, whom he also meant to find and take back with him. Then his plan became a lot less plausible.

He dismounted beyond the spring and went forward first afoot; it was not at all unusual for others to be resting there, and he did not wish to meet other travellers.

But the spring was deserted.

He brought forth his animal, turned it loose to drink deeply, then watched it turn greedily upon the ripgut and tules growing around the waterhole, which, any other time no horse would touch at all.

There were tracks in Borego Springs' soft, surrounding earth, which had been made since Conley's posse had been there. A few turned east and west, but mostly they pushed hurriedly on southward over the line. None of these tracks went north towards Sunflower and Conley's puckered eyes shone ironically at that; outlaws and night-riders did not ordinarily seek places where law and order existed.

This night, or what was left of it, Conley spent comfortably. He knew, as the desert-Indians also knew, that when the requisites to life were available a man should linger as long as he could making the most of them. Beyond every waterhole in the border country death in a dozen different guises was never more than arms distance away.

He tanked up on water, smoked peacefully with his lonely vision embracing the far-flung starshine which, on the desert, was the only companionship a man had, and he explored his earlier reflections; his thoughts with their unravelled ends brought up again by this powerful solitude.

His schedule was, thus far, as he'd planned it. A man like Dallas Benton might—probably would—ride over the line in broad daylight, but not Tim Conley. He knew this hostile land. He had learned early that nature, like Man, was not amenable to coercion, especially in this parched and merciless desert country. Those who survived here did not seek to force Nature to their will—nor the lawless breed of human beings who inhabited Nature's dry fastness either. They made it a rule of their lives to bend with Nature; to use her but never to coerce her.

In a thousand secret places lay the bones and mummies of men who had come south to challenge this eternal and unchanging land, dead not because Nature willed them so but dead by the hand of their own ignorance and arrogance.

Recalling now the words of Rose Bell, Conley disagreed that this was a 'lousy country'. It had in its own way been good to him. He knew it well. He understood its extravagant moods, its wildly flowing abundance in spring time and its teeming wintertime frostiness. But most important of all he understood its summertime sullenness, savagery and entrapping, villainous great patience when it caught the unwary, the foolish—like Dallas Benton—and the arrogant, grinding them between its twin evils of heat and aridity.

When Conley finally slept it was with the blacked-out total unconsciousness of a denned-up bear. He did not awaken for several hours, or until his built-in clock awakened him long after the moon was down.

He saddled up then and passed along on his continuing southward way to the U.S.-Mexican boundary, crossed it without knowing exactly where he'd done this, and kept on his lonely way.

Some time later, faintly discernible at the edge of the dark hush, a few pale stars low along Mexico's jagged horizon showed by their unwinking, steady burning that they were the lamps and sheltered candles of a village dead ahead.

Conley paused here to make a cigarette and smoke it while dredging deep into memory for his recollection of the way this village lay.

He had reached Nacori in the night as he'd planned to and somewhere on ahead a dreamlessly resting outlaw chieftain named Jeb Plummer did not know that a U.S. lawman had crossed over.

So far so good.

Conley finished the cigarette, killed it against his saddlehorn and raised the reins. For a time after he'd resumed his way he could make out neither buildings nor roadways, for such was the velvety quality of Mexican moonless nights that a man might ride into a slumbering town without knowing it, and this Conley had no wish at all to do in Nacori.

CHAPTER FIVE

Nacori lay in a swale of rolling countryside where shallow water had been found in earliest times by Mission Padres, so that in this one, exclusive area of desert, there were melon patches, green pastures, and irrigation ditches. Far out stood a mountain chain, hard and stiff against the paler night, and beyond those mountains was the breadth and depth of Mexico.

As Tim Conley approached the village in this half-light half-dark late hour a great depth of quiet lay over the place. There were no avenues in the sense that American towns had them, only casual alleyways making their way to, and beyond, the flat-roofed, single-storied adobe homes. Drying peppers hung colourfully from most buildings and muffling dust ankle-deep layered each roadway; an army could have passed through Nacori this night and no one would have heard its passing.

There was a liverybarn, run by an American whom Conley knew well, and out front of it was a spring-fed water-trough which overflowed constantly creating a deep mud-hole. During the hottest days pigs wandered here to lie motionless in the ooze with only snouts and eyes visible.

Nacori, like all Mexican towns, had a plaza. In the centre of this square, traditionally, stood the church. Also here, were clustered the stores, cantinas, little cafes, and vender-stands, for the plaza was Nacori's commercial heart.

Conley, shielded by the lateness and the gloom, made a complete circuit of the village, then rode beyond it into the countryside and there, where willows grew in great profusion, made a camp, turned loose his animal, lay back for a time resting, and shortly before dawn arose to go back afoot to the outskirts of Nacori and wait.

He had not slapped away the layered dust of travel, nor had he shaved or otherwise made himself presentable, and when he came out of nowhere to accost a woodcutter setting forth with his burros in the cool dawn, to get his daily allotment of faggots, the Mexican's eyes rolled and he crossed himself at the abrupt appearance of this frightening apparition.

'Rest tranquil,' said Conley in Spanish. 'I seek a man named Plummer. I mean no harm for you.'

The woodcutter hesitated. Conley read into this a reluctance on the man's part to speak of Plummer. Conley shifted position slightly and lay a hand upon his holstered hand-gun.

'*Si*,' said the woodcutter quickly. '*Señor* Plummer. Of course, *amigo*. He is in Nacori, yes. You are his friend, perhaps?'

'More than that,' replied Conley without prevaricating. 'I bring him great tidings.'

'He is at the *Cantina Libertad*. It is his headquarters, *Señor*.'

'*Gracias*,' said Conley. 'Thank you.'

'*Por nada*,' responded the Mexican and shortened the lead-rope to his animals. 'It is nothing.'

'One more question. Your name is what, *amigo*?'

To this the woodcutter said: 'Nemesis

Ybarra, *Señor.*' He watched Conley's face now, and saw the expression that appeared there; a steady-eyed consideration which said plainly that Conley would not forget Nemesis Ybarra. The woodcutter swallowed with some difficulty. A very deadly breed, these *Norte Americanos.*

'You are going into the hills after wood?' asked Conley now, his stare coldly speculative.

'*Si, Señor.*'

'For how long?'

'A day; perhaps two days, *Señor.*'

'It would be better, I think, if you remained away for a week, *amigo.* You could do this?'

'*Seguro,*' responded the woodcutter, having no difficulty in understanding this to be an order—and also a kind of threat.

Conley dipped into a trouser pocket, drew forth several gold coins and offered them to the woodcutter. 'A week then,' he said.

The Mexican took the coins and smiled broadly, his cupidity overshadowing his apprehension. 'One must go increasingly deeper into the hills for wood these days,' he said, and touched the brim of his sombrero. '*Adios, Americano.*'

Conley watched the woodcutter shuffle away; he had not wished for this man to noise it around Nacori that a stranger from above the border was seeking Plummer's gang, and while he had felt reasonably certain that the man would not do this anyway, because

Conley's appearance had very evidently struck fear into the Mexican, he was now quite sure the woodcutter would not return until he'd drunk up the money he'd received.

The *Cantina Libertad*, Conley knew, was Nacori's most popular saloon. It was owned by a cock-eyed Mexican of raffish appearance named Epifanio—'Pifas for short—Gomez. He knew 'Pifas Gomez quite well; had, in fact, once given him sanctuary in Sunflower when Gomez had had the poor taste of joining the side of a revolutionary junta which had fallen from favour and whose adherents had been zealously ferreted out and executed. But that had been years ago, and Tim Conley knew Mexicans too well to believe 'Pifas Gomez would still feel towards him any sentiments of gratitude, particularly if Plummer's gold was trickling into 'Pifas Gomez's hands, as it undoubtedly was.

Conley considered the eastward sky; there was as yet only darkness lying along the saw-toothed rims there, and yet he knew that dawn could not be far distant. Still, because necessity compelled him to do it, he struck out into Nacori in search of Dallas Benton, whom he knew would have arrived in the village no later than the afternoon before.

But, although Conley made a thorough search of the village, the liverybarn and every hitchrack, he found no evidence of Benton at all. Still, he told himself as he made his way

50

back to his camp in the willow-thicket, this did not mean Dallas Benton was not in Nacori. Actually, all it meant was that Dallas had not ridden guilelessly into the town, and Conley could draw some relief from this even though he still thought Benton too inexperienced to last long south of the border. Here, more than any other place Conley knew of, a stranger was noticed; Dallas Benton, for all his strong heart and burning wish for vengeance, would not, he thought, have the kind of canniness and sagacity it was required that a man have in Jeb Plummer's town.

Finally, because of nearing dawn and the fact that, since Conley wished not to draw attention to himself, there were many places he did not—dared not—enter in his search for Benton. He instead went into the willow thicket and remained there, a little hungry but at least not thirsty any more, until long after daylight came.

He strove to remember Gomez's saloon room by room. The *cantina* was not an elaborate building, yet it had, in conjunction with the bar, a series of small rooms used for gambling, for quartering travellers, and other purposes also. Conley had not been in Nacori in several years and he therefore had to concentrate strongly to recall how the saloon was appointed.

By mid-afternoon he thought he remembered the saloon's interior well enough;

all he had to do now was locate Burl Cassady, either in his room at the *cantina*, or in Nacori's byways, and also find Dallas Benton before Plummer did, and head north over the line in company with both men. He made a grimace. That was all he had to do.

He took out the picture Rose Bell had given him and lay for a long time studying each face, but particularly the features of Burl Cassady. It was not, he thought, the face of an intelligent man, yet neither did it have in either conformation or expression, the rabid look of a wanton killer. Cassady was, he mused, that typical gunman of the Southwest; a person gifted with superior co-ordination, which made him very deadly with a gun, and the absolute and total lack of ethics, scruples, or ideals, which separated good men from bad men. Cassady, riding over the body of the girl he'd shot, would not have gazed down with any feeling about what he'd done either way—no pity, no shame.

Conley mused for a while on other killers he'd known, but after a while, when this grew tiresome, he slept. Willow-shade hid him perfectly and somewhere northward, contentedly browsing, also dappled by willow-shade, his horse flicked flies and enjoyed his respite, after that gruelling desert crossing.

Late afternoon came and Conley, awakened as much by his hunger as by the completeness of his rest, sought a water-hole to wash at, then he went carefully to the extremity of his thicket and peered out. Nacori, not more than half a mile distant, appeared languidly alive with a little traffic passing in and out of the place. Beyond the town lay that expanse of northward desert Conley had recently traversed, and closer, were some wretched *jacals*—mud-wattle hovels—where Nacori's miserable existed. He cast an appraising glance skyward; dusk was not far off. Conley went back to look after his horse. By the time he'd finished here, there were broad shadows sweeping down over the land from those smoke-hazed distant mountains.

Conley left the thicket, made his way to one of the *jacals*, and there bought his fill of goat's milk and *tacos*, not exactly a rewarding diet, but for the time being an adequate one; Mexican armies since time out of mind had marched on as little and had accomplished as heroic feats as Tim Conley now entered darkening Nacori to do.

It was not difficult to remain unrecognised in the lowering dusk as long as he travelled only the back alleyways, which he did until he stood in that narrow space between Gomez's *Cantina Libertad* and the next adjoining adobe building. Here, Conley was in black shadows, his shoulders blending into dripping darkness. Beyond, where people shuffled past at the roadside, he was indistinguishable from the silence and the gloom which covered him.

From Gomez's saloon came a steady undertone of voices; the scraping of booted feet over the packed-earth floor, and the occasional clinking fall of chips or the soft music of glass upon glass.

Conley, with the additional handicap of not knowing the habits of the man he sought, composed himself to wait. He considered it likely that Cassady, like all his restless breed, would not be content to remain hour after hour within the same saloon, and this emergence into the roadway was what Conley now awaited.

He was confident that the Plummer gang had no inkling of his presence here in Nacori. He had only been here for one day, and that, he told himself, was about the extent of time any stranger could hope to elude all those suspicious and questioning glances with which Nacori abounded. He had, therefore, in order to minimise discovery and the certain death which would accompany disclosure, to make his move this very night. Perhaps, after he had gotten Cassady, he could spare a desperate two hours for the search of Nacori for Dallas Benton. But also, if anything untoward occurred, he would have to make a run for it with Cassady and return later for Benton. He reasoned in this way because he had long since accepted the death of Elizabeth Hardin as a fact.

A Mexican *vaquero* of willowy build came

out of Gomez's *cantina*, halted long enough to draw himself up with vast dignity, then walk northward past where Conley stood with a drunken man's extreme care. A moment later two more Mexican horsemen passed into the saloon and a little later an American loped up to the hitchrail, swung down, looped his reins and stood slapping desert dust off his clothing for a moment before passing beyond sight into the *cantina*.

Conley bent upon this man his quick and rummaging attention. The man, whose face was for the most part hidden as he bent to beat at the dust, was a dark-visaged man with a high, hooked nose and restless eyes. He was one of the men in the picture; Conley recalled his name without trouble: Buck Forsythe. Moments later a second recognisable outlaw rode up, got down and also passed into the saloon. This man, though, gave Conley no chance to recognise him, at least not fully, and the glimpse he caught, insufficient for positive identification, nevertheless inclined Conley to consider the man to be another Plummer outlaw, by the name of Kid Reilly.

It seemed to Conley that Plummer's gang was holding a rendezvous. The way the last two men had ridden up from opposite directions but almost at the same time, made him wonder if they had not been summoned for a meeting at a specific time. If this were so, then Jeb Plummer beyond doubt was planning another raid. Conley, recalling that Nacori had had no telegraph link with the Texas towns northward, found himself wondering if, since the last time he'd been here, this condition had been corrected. He doubted it; Mexican border villages changed very little from generation to generation, let alone from year to year.

One thing was quite certain; if Jeb Plummer was indeed planning another sortie, it would be over the line into Texas; he would not, for obvious reasons, jeopardise the safety he had in Nacori by raiding in Mexico.

Conley's excitement mounted as time passed. He was in a genuine dilemma. Unless he could get to a telegraph station and alert the border towns of Texas to the strong possibility of Plummer's coming, more women might die, more bullion might be stolen, and Plummer's renegades would escape again.

On the other hand, if he left Nacori now he might never again be able to enter this village and remain undetected, nor, for that matter, come so close to capturing Burl Cassady.

Finally, if he left now to spread the alarm, he would be compelled to abandon Dallas Benton, and Conley had no doubts at all about the fate which awaited Dallas.

There was a middle course, but its chances of success were slim indeed. But in the end, with night closing down wholly around him, Conley made his decision; it was a compromise, as most decisions are, and he was not keen about it. He would wait until about midnight using that time in an effort to apprehend Cassady and locate Dallas Benton, then, with or without these two he would head back for Sunflower and the telegraph office there, from which place he could warn the other border towns against Jeb Plummer's probable coming.

This was not a decision Conley enjoyed making; he had come a long way and had suffered considerably in order to get Cassady and Dallas Benton. He was now as close as he'd expected to get to total triumph—he was undetected in the midst of Plummer's town. And now he was being driven to abandon all this stealthy progress.

Because, he told himself, of nothing stronger than a suspicion. He felt bitter over this. Yet he had past records to go by; Plummer's undeviating method of operating for one thing, his ferocity, his speed of movement once he decided to move, and finally, his certain knowledge that whether he was right or wrong, it was still his moral obligation to warn the border villages so that other young girls would not be shot down in cold blood.

Jeb Plummer's record was graphically detailed in two respects. When he struck he did so with the suddenness of lightning; he wasted no time, ever, and he faded before pursuers like a wraith. Unless his victims had advance warning they stood absolutely no chance at all and Tim Conley knew this.

Plummer's second characteristic was utter ruthlessness. He never left a witness if he could avoid doing so; he operated in a military fashion except that he did not take prisoners as official guerrillas did; he executed them.

Finally, Jeb Plummer was an active renegade; he did not permit a lot of time to elapse between raids. Conley thought now wryly that the way Plummer and his riders spent gold they had to raid often. He also thought that it was time for Plummer to head out again; he was convinced that Plummer thoroughly meant to do this and that he had therefore and accordingly summoned his riders from their *ranchos* and homes to ride with him.

Conley passed his time now with a cigarette. He had made his decision and would abide by it, but he kept wondering if there was not still another way. Never before in his lifetime had he found himself in a position as difficult as this one; abandon a boy and a murderer in order to warn others, perhaps save the lives of people he did not know—all on the strength of nothing more than a strong suspicion.

Before he finished that cigarette Conley had promised himself something: If Plummer did not raid up over the line and Conley rode himself numb spreading a false alarm, and

58

afterwards returned to Nacori to find Dallas Benton dead, he would take up the trail of Burl Cassady and Jeb Plummer and follow it for as long as it took even though he had to resign his job as sheriff to do it; even though he spent the rest of his life pursuing two men whom he would kill.

Somewhere far out from where Conley was, a coyote made his sad, sad cry, its echo reaching deep inside Conley to find response in his heart-chords. He bent forward and very solemnly put out the cigarette.

CHAPTER SIX

Around Conley this mealy blackness of desert night clung to buildings as well as to the earth and sky. Lights shone weakly here and there, with the greatest number of lights coming from the *Cantina Libertad*, and with the passing of time more and more of Nacori's lights winked out until, a little before midnight, with increasing pressure upon Conley to seize the initiative and go in search of his man, almost the only lights along Nacori's main roadway came from the saloon.

A man left the *cantina* to halt a moment in the roadside dust. He smoked, and little fitful bursts of sullen glow showed at his cigarette's tip. He looked leisurely up the roadway and down it, then arced away the cigarette, strode to the hitchrack, caught at his reins and stepped across a saddled animal. Conley, straining to see this man's face, recognised him as the outlaw he'd earlier thought was Kid Reilly. This man appeared in no hurry as he wheeled clear of the rack and started southward through the night. Then stillness returned.

It was midnight, and Conley was about to abandon his vigil, when the second outlaw appeared. This was Buck Forsythe, and as he went stolidly towards his mount Conley considered accosting him, determining where Burl Cassady was, and going after him. Then, as Forsythe swung his horse and rose up to settle across the saddle, a third outlaw came swiftly through the saloon's doorway to call softly ahead, saying: 'Hey, Buck; just a minute.'

Forsythe halted, loosening the reins and gazing downward. The second dark figure moved forward to stop beside him.

'You figurin' on usin' that apaloosa horse tomorrow night?'

Forsythe seemed to consider this question before replying. Then he said, 'Hell, Burl; you got the savinna the same time I got the apaloosa. Why don't you use him?'

Forsythe had evidently correctly guessed what his friend had been about to ask, because now the second man settled back upon his heels, saying, 'He ain't as fast—that's why. Are you goin' to use him or not?'

'I thought I might,' answered the mounted man.

'But you got this big chestnut, and he's tougher'n a boiled owl. You don't need the apaloosa.'

'I used this horse on that Sunflower raid an' I don't like to use any of 'em twice in a row.' Forsythe grew meditative. He finally shrugged and said, 'All right; you can use the apaloosa.' Then paused a moment before adding, 'But Burl; he ain't very well reined.'

'All I'll need is speed,' said the man on the ground. 'We won't be roping no calves.' He chuckled softly, but this sound carried to Conley's ears through the nightly hush. 'I'll trade you a couple of my other critters for him.'

'No,' exclaimed Forsythe, shortening his reins again and beginning to turn away. 'He's the first one of them spotted-rumped horses I ever owned. I'll keep him—at least for a while.' Forsythe bobbed his head. 'See you tomorrow night, Burl. *Adios.*'

'Yeah,' agreed Cassady. '*Adios.*'

Conley glided forward until he stood only inches from the *Cantina Libertad*'s front wall. He rested one palm against the rough, rammed earth wall and watched Buck Forsythe walk his horse northward, then, timing it perfectly, he took two forward steps

61

as Forsythe faded out in blackness, and also as Burl Cassady turned back the way he had come.

Cassady did not at once understand he was not alone, but when this realisation came the outlaw appeared curious rather than alarmed. He peered at Conley's vague silhouette saying '*Quién es?*' as though Conley were a Mexican.

The reply Cassady got back came at him even and very hard. It turned him to stone there in the yellow-orange outflow of lamp light from the *Cantina Libertad*.

'Walk over where I am, Cassady, and keep both your hands ahead of you!'

The outlaw seemed to have trouble believing he was being challenged in Nacori; he moved out as Conley had directed, but only after an interval of long hesitation.

When he was close, Conley pushed his pistol barrel into Cassady's soft parts and herded him by this pressure into the narrow place between buildings where he'd stood for so long. There, without another word passing between them, Conley plucked away Cassady's holstered belt-gun and pushed him roughly face forward against an adobe wall.

'I got no hide-outs,' said the outlaw, speaking for the first time. 'Who the hell are you, anyway?'

'Never mind,' responded Conley, beginning to run his free hand over Cassady's body feeling for secreted weapons—called hide-

62

outs.

Then, as though abruptly jarred away from astonishment and for the first time fully realising his peril and reacting to it, Burl Cassady flung about with great speed and lashed out as he did so. Conley, a little off balance, was caught high on the right shoulder by Cassady's looping blow and had to stagger to retain balance. He had no time for using his gun; Cassady drove into him with desperation and flailing arms. A wild blow caught Conley across the bridge of the nose, and that one brought up tears.

Conley let off a curse, spun clear, dropped his pistol and brought up both fists. Cassady, still pushing, bent his knees and churned forward low and fast. Conley aimed a savage blow and missed. The renegade's shoulderpoint caught him in the chest carrying him back against the *cantina*'s rough wall and Cassady struck him three times hard in the middle. None of these blows had great power behind them, but they kept Conley from striking back.

Behind them their elongated shadows danced wildly upon the far wall. Then one shadow lurched back and swooped low. Conley, seeing Cassady dive for the dropped six-gun, hurled himself upon the younger man. One hundred and eighty pounds of bone and gristle struck Cassady head-on; the outlaw was knocked flying. He fetched up against that far wall where their shadows had been and a great sob burst past his lips. Then Conley was on him, granite fists striking solidly where Cassady was suspended against the wall unable to get clear.

The outlaw closed; locked his arms about Conley to smother those punishing fists with his body, and the two of them heaved and staggered and wrestled along the wall in panting silence. Conley, unable to break Cassady's hold with his arms, brought up a knee with great force and Cassady's arms flew wide; a whimper burst past his lips and he doubled over lurching clear. Conley paused only long enough to flex his arms, then he moved in with a forward step and brought up a solid strike from near the ground. It caught the outlaw flush along the jaw straightening him up to his full height, where he hung only briefly, arms to his sides, eyes turning far back into his skull, then Burl Cassady toppled backwards, struck the earth all loose and sodden, and did not move.

Conley went back for his gun. He also found Cassady's weapon and shoved it into the waistband of his levis. After that he returned to Cassady's side and stood there gulping in lungsful of the heavy night air; taking each inhalation to the very bottom of his lungs while the thunder of his rocketing heart beat solidly inside his head.

Around him Nacori was as before, quietly,

64

serenely dark and peaceful. Conley bent, after a little time had passed, grasped Burl Cassady by one shoulder, and heaved him upright. The outlaw gasped and put both hands pressingly to his midriff. He hung in Conley's grip for several moments more, before compelling himself to straighten up out of this crouch. Then he shook his head—but gingerly, as though it were a fishbowl filled to the brim. Conley's voice, as even and hard as before, expedited his return to normalcy.

'Where is your horse?'

'At—the liverybarn.'

'That's too bad,' said the lawman dryly. 'Because we're not going in there.' He let his hold on Cassady relax. 'I reckon we'll just have to appropriate one of the horses at the hitchrack.'

'Who—the hell—are you, anyway?' Asked the renegade, twisting for a close look at Conley.

'I'm the law in Sunflower, sonny. I also happen to be a sort of uncle to that girl you shot up there.'

Cassady's head cleared now, completely. His gaze turned slate-black with both understanding and fear. 'Naw,' he began to protest. 'I didn't shoot no girl in—'

'Oh, shut up and pick up your hat,' growled Conley, giving Cassady a slight shove towards the crushed hat where it lay in the trampled dust. 'And don't yell out—or I'll blow your brains out.'

Cassady retrieved his headgear and as he donned it his face assumed a ferret-like look of quick concentration. 'Wait a minute,' he said to Conley. 'You'll never get me clear of Nacori.'

'I'll have to take that chance,' replied the lawman, stopping beside Cassady. Then he added: 'But I'll tell you one thing: if I don't make it, sonny, neither will you.'

'I'll make a bargain with you.'

'You couldn't trade me a bucket of water if I was dyin' of thirst,' said Conley, giving the renegade another little push. 'Go on; head down this alley.'

'Listen a minute,' protested Cassady. 'There's a feller here from Sunflower ...'

Conley ceased moving. His scorning gaze held to Cassady's face. In a low tone he said, 'Describe him.'

'He's about my age. About my height too. I didn't pay much attention when they brought him in, but I think his name is Dallas something-or-other.'

Conley nodded as though this came as no surprise to him. 'Where is he?'

'Jeb had him put in the local *calabozo*.'

'Jeb must be the law hereabouts,' said Conley. 'All right; where is this jail?'

Cassady stared. 'You ain't thinkin' of bustin him out,' he exclaimed, making a statement of it.

66

'I had that in mind, yes.'

Cassady began to smile slowly. 'Good idea,' he said. 'Come on, I'll show you.'

'You'll do better than that,' growled Conley. 'You'll go up to the door and tell whoever is guarding him to come outside.'

Now Cassady's smile died away. 'Not me,' he ground out swiftly. 'Pete Bravo's his guard.'

Conley, sensing from the way Cassady had said this that Pete Bravo, whoever he was, was a man to be feared, exclaimed: 'You can take your choice; my gun or his.'

Cassady twisted; he screwed up his face; the ferret-look returned. 'He'll shoot at the drop of a hat, man. Even I couldn't walk in there tonight.'

'You're going to walk in there, Cassady, so let's get started.'

The renegade considered Conley's dead-level and icy gaze. He flinched from the lawman's look saying, 'What d'you want this feller for; he's just a tomfool who come ridin' up behind town in broad daylight and got caught flat-footed. You want to get killed over a man like that?'

'If I got to make a choice,' replied Conley wryly, 'then I'd rather get it over a man like him—than a man like you. Now get going.' Conley strode forward and raised his hand.

Cassady wheeled away muttering over his shoulder. 'Pete's half drunk, lawman. When he's like that he'd shoot his own mother.

That's why Jeb put him to guardin' that feller; to keep him out o' the streets.'

Conley heard, but moved through the pitch darkness without comment. They walked southward through refuse-laden back alleyways and across stony patches of ground between buildings until, near the far end of Nacori, Cassady halted where the desert began, and pointed across the yonder roadway.

'There. That little 'dobe building off by itself. That's the *calabozo*—the jailhouse.'

Cassady's arm fell away; he turned to fix a sly look upon Tim Conley, waiting. Conley studied the jailhouse for a long time without speaking. It was an ugly, square, and functional building which had been built with walls three feet thick, only one oaken door, and beside that massive door, a solitary steel-barred little window. It resembled a small fortress, and, reflected Conley, if he'd ever seen an impregnable building before in his lifetime, it could not have been any more assault-proof than this squatting structure was.

He felt like swearing; time was passing; he would very shortly now have to abandon Nacori, yet here he was, tantalisingly close to accomplishing all that he'd hoped to accomplish including the finding of Dallas Benton, faced now by an impregnable building guarded by a madman.

He said to Cassady: 'Tell me how Jeb Plummer would get inside there.'

'He wouldn't,' came the immediate reply. 'Jeb would wait until morning because all of us who know Pete Bravo know what he'll do if anyone—even Jeb himself—tries to enter that there *calabozo* until Pete's sobered-up again.'

Conley turned, scowling. 'You mean to tell me this Bravo is so trigger-happy he'll shoot anyone when he's been drinking.'

'Lawman,' Cassady stated flatly, 'that's exactly what I'm telling you. When he's drinkin' Pete Bravo's *loco*—insane—crazy; whatever you want to call it. He can't talk sense and he can't think sense. I'd as soon step on a rattlesnake with my bare feet as go up to Pete when he's liquored-up.'

Conley's scowl deepened. He returned his attention to the jailhouse. How did you get inside a place built as that building was, get past, around, or over, a drunken maniac, and release a prisoner—all without any shooting, any noise?'

Moments passed. Conley did not move but Cassady did; he made a very faint chuckle. Conley turned on him.

'Don't laugh just yet,' he said flintily. 'I've still got you.'

Cassady's smile died out. He stood silently thoughtful and not until Conley spoke again did he return his eyes to the lawman's face.

'Start walking,' said Conley curtly. 'Head out across the road.'

'To the jailhouse?'

69

'Yes, to the jailhouse, and don't make any noise either. Get going.'

But the renegade's face, gone suddenly ashen, continued there beside Conley. 'Listen,' Cassady husked. 'Listen a minute, Sheriff. He'll shoot. I swear it—he'll shoot to kill.'

'If he's drunk enough maybe he'll miss,' growled Conley, who reached up and gave the outlaw a rough push. 'Go on.'

'The noise will bring Jeb and the others,' stated Cassady, speaking so swiftly the words blurred all together, stumbling forward under Conley's repeated shoving.

'We'll have to take that chance. Now shut up.'

They passed over the dark and empty roadway almost side by side and stopped in the lee of Nacori's jailhouse.

Tim Conley cast a slow, appraising glance over the darkly massive building in front of them. 'What did they originally build this thing for—Indian attacks?'

Burl Cassady said not a word. He was sweating; reflected night-light shone glisteningly off his face. When he finally spoke his voice was a low whisper.

'Keep quiet,' he said. 'He might hear you. Listen, lawman, what I told you is the gospel truth. There isn't any way to get in there without getting us both killed.'

Conley, in a lowered voice, said, 'I don't think I want to get in there, Cassady.'

The outlaw looked enormously relieved. 'Then let's get t'hell away from here—and quick.'

But Conley shook his head. An idea had come to him. Gaining access to the jailhouse being out of the question, there remained but one way to liberate Dallas Benton. Conley had been a lawman a long time; he had, over the years, encountered just about every variety of misfit that inhabited the border country. From this experience he'd learned one thing: There was a way to handle all people, even madmen, even insane drunks such as Pete Bravo, but you had to know the secret—and this was, succinctly, to appeal to them where they had the most feeling.

CHAPTER SEVEN

While Cassady watched from a distance of less than four feet Conley went boldly to the door of the Nacori jailhouse and rapped with his pistol barrel, calling forth as he did so: 'Pete; I got a bottle of *tequila* for you.'

Conley then cocked his head listening, and looked up at Cassady as heavy footfalls approached the door from within. 'Come up close,' said Conley, gesturing with his six-gun. Cassady obeyed, but with strong reluctance. 'Now stand here,' he ordered.

'He'll shoot,' bleated the outlaw.

Conley shrugged. 'Maybe. But he's not too drunk to think someone's out here with a free bottle of liquor for him.'

The door-bolts rattled. Conley went up close to the building and flattened there, his gun up and cocked. He was hoping mightily that there would be no exchange of shots, and in order to preclude this strong possibility, as the door began to open he raised his gun-hand high.

A massive, shock-headed man stood wide-legged in the doorway peering out. He seemed, in that first glimpse Conley had of him, to be some kind of a throw-back; some rare and terrible phantom of prehistoric man. His arms hung inordinately long at his sides and his skull rode forward upon powerful shoulders. The man seemed to have no neck at all.

Burl Cassady stood as though rooted. He bleated something. The shaggy, back-grounded silhouette in the doorway made an answering snarl from deep in his throat—and Conley struck.

Pete Bravo was caught just over the right ear by Conley's blow. He staggered back into the room struggling mightily to retain his balance. In a second Conley lunged forward, grabbed Cassady and hurled him into the jailhouse and sprang in behind him. Bravo was beginning to wilt, but it took him a long time to crumple. When he finally did collapse, it was to strike the packed-earth floor with a soft-rustling sound. He let off one ragged breath and flattened.

'*Sheriff!*'

Conley looked across at the solitary cell. Dallas Benton was rigidly standing there, both arms up, both hands gripping the bars with great force.

Without acknowledging Benton's greeting, Conley gestured towards a wall-peg with his six-gun. 'Get those keys hanging there,' he ordered Cassady, 'and turn him loose.'

Cassady obeyed silently, still pale from the experience he'd just lived through. Dallas Benton, scarcely wasting a glance on the outlaw, pushed clear of his cell and made a relieved smile at Conley. 'How did you ever get here?' he asked.

To this Conley made no response either. He said only: 'Where is your gun?'

'In that desk,' replied Benton, indicating a scarred piece of furniture.

'Get it, boy, and put it on. Then disarm this ape on the floor and let's get riding. We've got a heap of ground to cover before sunup.'

As Benton moved swiftly past, Conley eyed Cassady. 'One thing to remember,' he said to the bandit. 'A whisky guzzler'll do anything to anyone—but he won't hurt the source of his supply.' He motioned towards the door. 'Lead out for the nearest hitchrack where there are saddled horses.'

The three of them emerged from Nacori's jailhouse into layers of blackness. When Dallas Benton would have spoken Conley silenced him with the same snarl he'd used on Cassady.

'Plenty of time to talk later. For now, just shut up and keep your eyes peeled.'

Conley would have led them to Gomez's *Cantina Libertad* but three buildings south where a smaller saloon stood, there also were drowsing saddle animals, and here Conley herded his two companions, ordered them astride, then took a horse himself, and led out northward in a stiff trot, keeping Burl Cassady at his side and under his gun.

Beyond Nacori he slowed, let off a great sigh of relief, and cut easterly. At this, both Cassady and Dallas Benton looked surprised. Conley offered no explanation until he was back where his horse was, then, abandoning the stolen animal and rigging-out his own horse, Conley got back into the saddle and motioned for Cassady to lead out northerly around Nacori and into the pitch black desert-night beyond.

After two miles of steady riding Conley slowed, put up his six-gun and twisted up a cigarette. With reins looped around his saddlehorn, Conley dragged back a great gust of smoke, and slowly, savouringly, expelled it. 'God damn,' he solemnly said, 'it's good to be alive.' Then his mood changed and he fixed

74

Dallas Benton with a look. 'You fool. You damned young pup. I ought to whale the tar out of you for headin' down this way like you did.'

Benton coloured but it was too dark for Conley to notice this. He said: 'Some fool of a Mex came onto me when I was watering my horse and ran to tell Plummer. They had me surrounded in a wink of an eye.'

'The Mex wasn't the fool,' stated Conley. 'You were. I thought even a pup like you would have better sense than to ride into Nacori in broad daylight.'

Benton glared at Cassady's back, on ahead, saying nothing to this. Conley continued speaking.

'I don't know why they took you alive. Strangers aren't usually treated so kindly down here in Jeb Plummer's town. Tell me something, Dallas: Just what did you expect to accomplish here, anyway?'

'Get Plummer.'

'Plummer didn't shoot Elizabeth.'

'No? Well; he'd have done for me as a starter.'

At this remark Conley's brows climbed. He said: 'Always best to start with the worst one, isn't it?' Then he snorted. 'Jeb Plummer would've gunned you down with one hand and tossed off a drink while he was doing it.'

This accolade to Plummer's gun-prowess brought an exclamation from Burl Cassady.

'He will yet, too. You two just think you're out of the woods, but you sure as hell ain't.'

Dallas scowled forward at Cassady but Sheriff Conley turned a thoughtfully speculative look upon his prisoner. For a while he jogged along silently, then he said: 'By sunup Plummer'll have our tracks to go by—but he's not foolish enough to try this desert crossing in full daylight.'

'Neither,' said Cassady sharply, 'are you.'

They made it to Borego Springs by dawn's first pale lighting, startled a watering band of prong-horn antelope, tanked up their horses, filled Conley's canteen, the only container they had among them, then slowly swelled up with water themselves, and Conley ordered the retreat resumed.

Now Cassady protested again; this time with logic on his side. 'You crazy or something?' He irately demanded of Conley. 'We can't ride out through here in daylight. That damned sun'll fry all our brains before afternoon.'

Conley reached up, tugged forward his hatbrim to shield his eyes, and said only two words: 'Ride on!'

Cassady obeyed, but his expression was at first glum, then, five miles farther on with sizzling heat jumping up from mica-particles in the earth to hurt his eyes, he croaked. 'I'm dry already.'

'Stick a coin in your mouth,' growled Conley. 'And keep on riding.'

76

Dallas Benton, silent for so long, turned finally to gaze fully upon Conley. From dry and cracking lips he said, 'A while back you said it wasn't Jeb Plummer who shot Elizabeth.'

'That's right. It wasn't Plummer.'

'If you're so sure of that, Sheriff, you must know who it was.'

Conley rocked along saying nothing. From the corner of his narrowed gaze he sighted Cassady watching him from a beet-red face.

'Who was it, Sheriff?'

'Never mind,' answered Conley. 'When the time comes I'll tell you. Until then just concentrate on favouring your horse and getting through this day alive.'

'I want to know!'

Conley bent a long, narrowed gaze at the man beside him. It was a look which spoke volumes; no words went with it, and no words had to. Dallas Benton understood clearly enough. Conley was not going to name Elizabeth's assassin.

Onward flowed the pure flare of desert, desolate, endlessly silent, and more deadly than any other kind of country anywhere on earth. There arose a blue blur in the far distance and overhead a steely sky held its molten yellow disc. Hours passed, powder-fine dust arose to mantle the three silent riders, and after a time the alkali in this same dust pained the eyes, stung the nostrils, and scorched the throat.

Cassady called for a drink of water before noon. Conley threw him a disdaining look and rode on. By one o'clock Cassady's protests assumed an almost desperate pleading. Finally, where three paloverdes grew together and a watery kind of diluted shade lay, Conley drew up and got down. Dallas Benton and Cassady tumbled off too and flung themselves down in this shade. Conley led all three animals in out of the fierce brightness and attended to them; loosened their cinches, held aloft each saddle for air to pass over sweating backs, then he moistened his handkerchief with water from the canteen and washed out the mouth of each horse. He afterwards passed deeper into the shade, sank down with the canteen at his side, and made a cigarette. When this was going satisfactorily, he swept his burning eyes to Dallas Benton.

'Want a drink?' he asked, and when Benton nodded Conley passed him the canteen.

Burl Cassady watched all this from hating, red and sunken eyes. Conley smoked on, waiting for Benton's gulpings to come, and when they did, he watched the outlaw.

Cassady's fingers curled deep into the sandy soil, his tongue made a swift and darting circuit of his parched lips. He swore at Conley, seeing the lawman's gaze upon him.

'Save your energy,' exclaimed the lawman quietly. 'You just might make it back—if you do.'

'You're figurin' on lettin' me die out here,' cried Cassady. He swore at Conley, calling him any name which came to mind.

Benton finished drinking, capped the canteen and looked across at Conley, hesitating. It was clearly in his mind that Conley's torturing of his prisoner was deliberate and inhuman.

Conley, meeting this gaze and reading it aright, extended his hand. Benton put the canteen in it and looked away.

Conley then turned towards Cassady saying, 'How bad do you want a drink?'

Cassady's cursing broke off. He stared. There was a flicker of hope in his look. Then it died and he ranted again, accusing the lawman of deliberately doing this; saying Conley had no intention of giving him water.

To all this Conley appeared deaf until Cassady broke off, panting and glaring. Then he spoke quietly, saying, 'I ought to do all those things to you, Cassady, but I won't because I don't want to be an animal like you are.' He held up the canteen. 'You can have a drink. But first you'll have to tell me where Plummer is riding tonight.'

The renegade's filthy hand went up to push sweat across his face. He stared at the canteen. 'Sunflower,' he croaked. 'He's leadin' the gang to Sunflower again.'

Conley lowered the canteen to his lap. He

considered the panting, tormented man's face. Then without questioning this seeming prevarication, he handed Cassady the canteen and looked away as the outlaw slavered in his shaking eagerness.

To Benton the sheriff said, 'A coyote will risk repeating himself, but damned few other animals will. The coyote is smart enough to know that folks never expect lightning to strike twice in the same place.' Conley punched out his cigarette, reached over and wrenched the canteen from Cassady's lips. 'You can kill yourself drinking like that in this heat,' he exclaimed dispassionately. 'Besides; this has to last until we get where we're going.'

Dallas Benton was watching the outlaw with an expression of pure disbelief across his features. 'You're a liar,' he finally said to Cassady. 'I don't care what the sheriff thinks—I say you're a liar.'

'No,' gasped the outlaw, catching his breath after that wild gulping of tepid water. 'No; it's the gospel truth. He's ridin' for Sunflower. I'm not lyin' to you.'

Benton swung towards the lawman. 'Why? Why would Plummer try it again so soon? Is there another load of bullion comin' in on one of the stages? It'd have to be something as good as that to make him risk it—*if* he's really planning to risk it.'

'No,' said Conley, 'there's no more bullion coming in.' He capped the canteen then arose to stand motionless hearkening to the southerly wastes. No sounds came to him from that direction. He relaxed to stand thoughtful for a time, then slung the canteen over his shoulder and considered Dallas Benton seeking signs of exhaustion, of lethargy. Finding none he turned towards the horses.

'Reckon your friends aren't coming after all,' he drawled to Cassady. 'Not a sound anywhere.'

Cassady arose. He started to speak when Dallas Benton cut across his forming words. Dallas was frowning in puzzlement.

'Why, Sheriff? I'd like to know what's in Sunflower that'd make Jeb Plummer try another raid up there. It doesn't make sense; surely he knows folks're still all roiled up over his last raid.'

'That probably doesn't worry him much,' said Conley. 'A man like Plummer who has had a lot of success gets contemptuous after a while. And maybe he's had reason. Lord knows he's been around long enough and no one's yet put a rope on him.'

'Nor will they,' snapped Burl Cassady. 'You can bet your lousy bottom dollar on that.'

Dallas turned a fiery look upon the outlaw and Cassady wilted before it saying no more.

'Then,' said Dallas, 'he's getting near the end of his rope, for no outlaw in his right mind raids a town just for the hell of raiding it.'

'Plummer wouldn't do that,' Conley replied.

'He's no fool.'

'Why, then?' demanded Dallas again. 'If there's no bullion and he isn't making this raid out of pure cussedness—why is he making it?'

'The bank,' murmured Conley. 'Now quit talkin' and get astride.' He turned. 'Give Cassady a hand there.'

There was now sluggishness to the movements of men and animals. It was heat-induced and although neither the horses nor the horsemen were yet actually in peril this was the first indication that the draining of their wills and their resolves was slowly and inexorably overtaking them.

Sometimes men went for endless hours like this; other times they bore up less stubbornly and this was what troubled Conley now. He knew that he, himself, could endure and survive, but he could not gauge the depth of toughness in his companions. Oftentimes men whose exteriors showed the greatest promise of durability were the first to collapse under a burning sun in this land where sweat dried between skin and shirt. You never knew until it was too late to turn back, exactly how other men would stand up under a heat so scalding that you could fry eggs to a crisp on any exposed boulder, and of course by that time it was usually too late to succour them.

The solution of course was to travel only at night. For obvious reasons this was not feasible now, and Conley, realising fully that this was so, kept a secretively watchful eye upon both Benton and Burl Cassady. If either failed now, rather than burden their already over-ridden horses, which would result in all of them being set afoot, the failing man would have to be abandoned, and this of course meant certain death.

The way of the transgressor, he told himself wryly, was indeed hard—but the way of the lawman who went after the transgressor was even harder.

CHAPTER EIGHT

The afternoon wore along, the heat of it an actual physical force that men and animals had to lean into. It danced ahead in such a way that to the three sun-blackened riders there appeared to be a void space between the desert verdure and the actual ground itself.

Above, a malignant orange disc was falling away westerly, its slanting rays blindingly intense and dehydrating. Conley rode easy in the saddle scarcely moving, his eyes pinched nearly closed and his tough-set lips drooping slightly downwards at their outer corners. At his side Dallas Benton slouched along in glum silence, only occasionally flicking a glance at either Conley or Burl Cassady.

It was the outlaw who seemed to be

suffering most. He reeled in the saddle and, because he'd initially licked his lips when the heat had come upon them, he now had to continue this, because otherwise, had he stopped, his lips would have swollen to twice actual size, then cracked and bled.

Conley thought that what made this desert crossing so particularly hard on Cassady was the life he'd led. It helped greatly if a man was in good physical shape when he tackled a desert, and very clearly Cassady was not in this kind of shape. He perspired easily, as did most men who drank heavily, and, because he'd obviously avoided sleep lately, he now rode along loose and drooping, almost reeling out of the saddle now and then.

Conley made a second halt when the sun was well off meridian; falling away towards the heat-hazed west so that what thin shade there was, lay easterly. Two immense barrel cacti were their backdrops this time. Dallas Benton, remembering Conley's earlier concern for their animals, cared for his beast when he'd dismounted. So did Tim Conley; but Burl Cassady simply dismounted and wilted low upon the ground leaving this chore for the sheriff. Afterwards, they sat in a kind of stupor-induced lethargy, silent until Benton asked how much farther it was to Sunflower.

'Ought to get there about midnight,' answered the lawman. 'Give or take an hour.'

Cassady stirred at the sound of voices.

'Water,' he croaked.

Conley lifted the canteen, shook it close to his head and glanced across at Benton. 'Make it last,' he said, extending the canteen. Benton drank sparingly and returned the container. Again Conley shook it.

'You haven't had any,' said Benton.

Conley did not reply to this. He glanced at Cassady, saying: 'Why did you boys leave Sunflower after you robbed the stage; why didn't you rob the bank then, too?'

Cassady was peering desperately from beneath his tugged-down hatbrim at the canteen. He understood what Conley was doing. As before, Cassady would get the drink he had to have, but only after answering questions.

'Because, after we'd hit the stage and was ridin' off—without our masks on—we come onto this girl. She got a real good look at all o' us.'

'But,' said Conley, 'you shot her—left her for dead. She couldn't have returned to town in time to warn anyone about you.'

'Jeb said we dassn't chance it.' Cassady straightened up. 'If anything went wrong we couldn't have gotten away. You see, we had it figured to hit the stage an' the bank before sundown. That way we could've ridden south into this damned desert and had all night to get clear of a posse. By hard ridin' we'd have been at the Springs the next mornin' an' if a

85

posse'd come after us—they'd have had to cross in broad daylight, which no one in their right senses would do, or wait until the next night. By that time we'd be over the line.'

Dallas Benton began to nod. 'Plummer's no fool,' he said.

Conley agreed. 'That's one thing no one's ever accused him of being. Fools in his business don't last long and Plummer's been around a long time.'

'Do I get the drink now?'

Conley wordlessly passed over the canteen, waited until Cassady had gulped several mouthfuls, then jerked it away from him. Cassady swore. 'That ain't enough to keep a lousy bird alive,' he said. Conley capped the canteen with finality without looking away from the outlaw.

'I'd give more to a bird,' said he; then started to work up a cigarette.

For a time Cassady watched this operation, then he smiled. 'You think you're pretty clever, ridin' into Nacori and catchin' me, don't you?'

Conley lit up, exhaled and offered the sack to Dallas Benton without paying any additional attention to Cassady.

'Pretty soon now you're goin' to find out you ain't smart at all, Sheriff.'

Something akin to exultation in the renegade's tone brought Conley's gaze around. He considered Cassady's bitter smile for a time, then shrugged. 'I never claimed to be smart,' he said, 'only persevering. In this case I think that'll be enough.'

'You're wrong, Conley. You're wrong as all hell. Perseverin's only goin' to get you killed.' Cassady's smile began to firm up with a genuine kind of crafty amusement. 'Because, when you said Jeb was no fool, you only half described him. He's smart as a whip. He's already got you out-guessed.'

Conley smoked on saying nothing. Cassady knew something, he was confident of that, and he also knew that he could winnow it out of the outlaw with more water. The trouble was, the half-canteen which was left had to last the three of them the rest of the way to Sunflower and if Cassady got more of it than he or Dallas got, it was very possible that Cassady would be the only one who finished the desert crossing.

While Conley was thinking, Dallas said, 'Plummer can't catch us now.' He directed this to Cassady. 'You said yourself he's too smart to try a daylight crossing.'

'He doesn't have to try that to beat the sheriff, here,' gloated Cassady, who evidently was drawing considerable satisfaction from Conley's pensive expression.

'You're talkin' like an idiot,' growled Dallas Benton. 'A plumb idiot.'

'Am I?' retorted the outlaw. He leaned forward a little to give his next words emphasis. 'Well; let me tell you two smart *hombres* something. Last night there was a meetin' in Nacori. All Jeb's gang was there. He told us we'd be ridin' to Sunflower again.'

'We already know that,' said Benton dourly.

'Sure you do. What you don't know—you two smart fellers—is that Jeb never makes a raid without carefully scoutin' out the lay o' the land first.'

'What's that got to do with it?' challenged Benton.

Conley's head began to lift slowly; his eyes swung from their thoughtful consideration of the ground at his feet to grow steady upon Cassady's face. He had already surmised what Cassady's answer was going to be.

'Last night,' said Cassady, enunciating each word with particular clarity, as though he enjoyed making this statement, 'Jeb sent Kid Reilly and Buck Forsythe on ahead to scout-up the countryside around Sunflower.'

Benton sat without moving. Tim Conley, who had guessed this was what the outlaw was going to relate, was lost in thought again. Cassady made a little, harsh laugh.

'The Kid and Buck had all last night to get on ahead of us. They both know this damned desert and every foot of ground beyond it, too.' Cassady looked from Benton to Conley, his smile broadly lingering. 'They're to come south and meet Jeb an' the rest of the crew and lead 'em on in for the raid. So— you smart-alecks—you aren't out-ridin' the Plummer gang at all. What you're really doin' is ridin' right smack in between two parts of the gang.'

Benton, too, turned his attention upon the sheriff. 'He's lying,' he exclaimed to Conley.

But the lawman, who had seen both Forsythe and Reilly leave Nacori, shook his head. 'No; it's the truth, Dallas. But he's makin' it out a lot worse than it is.'

'How?' challenged Cassady instantly. 'You tell me how I'm makin' it worse?'

'Forsythe and Reilly don't know we're comin',' said Conley. 'They may see us—if there's enough moonlight—but they won't know whether we're Plummer or us.'

'Like hell they won't,' hooted Cassady. 'They'll know.'

'Maybe,' conceded Conley laconically. 'But we'll have the advantage, Cassady, they won't. We know they're on ahead somewhere, so we'll be watchin' and ready. They won't.'

Cassady turned this over in his mind. His expression altered away from its previous exultation. 'Maybe you don't think you'll get caught between two fires,' he snarled.

'That doesn't worry me at all,' answered the lawman. 'Plummer's not going to be that close behind us. We've got a long lead on him. Remember; you said he was too smart to attempt a daylight crossing.' Conley arose, threw a look outward where the sun was dropping away, then jerked his head at the two seated men. 'Let's go,' he ordered tersely, and started forward towards his horse.

They were moving away from their two big barrel cacti when Conley spoke forward to Cassady. 'If you hadn't just had to prove how smart Plummer was, maybe we'd have ridden into Forsythe and Reilly. Sometimes a big mouth is a heap more deadly than a gun, Cassady.'

The outlaw threw Conley a hard look over his shoulder but said nothing.

They passed along over the dusty ground with little clouds of alkali powder scuffed to life beneath their horses' hooves; with the slanting sun-rays burning fully against their left sides, and with the stifling heat as oppressive as ever although it was now late in the afternoon.

Dallas Benton, assessing the sun's gradual descent, said bitterly, 'I wish, for once, summer sunlight didn't last so damned long.'

'Nine o'clock,' exclaimed Conley, without looking around. 'It won't be dark now until nine o'clock.'

Benton considered this, then asked the obvious question. 'You reckon Forsythe and Reilly could make their scout around Sunflower and start back down this way before sundown?'

Conley had already weighed this possibility, and now shook his head. 'They didn't have more than an hour's lead on us. At the most two hours. My guess is that even if they pushed their horses hard; kept on riding after sunup this morning; they still would be only sighting Sunflower at just about this hour.'

Conley cocked an eye at the sun. Benton, too, regarded the lowering disc. For a time neither of them spoke, then Conley said, 'It'll take them at least another hour, maybe more, to make certain Sunflower's safe for the gang to hit tonight. Then add another hour or such a matter, to ride back down as far as we've come northward, and by then it's going to be pretty doggone late, Dallas.'

'Good,' said Benton. 'I didn't cherish the idea of being spotted by them first.' Dallas turned a lingering look upon Cassady, who was shuffling along a hundred feet or so ahead. 'You reckon he's got it figured out where Forsythe and Reilly will cross our trail?'

Conley shrugged. 'Maybe. It doesn't matter as long as he keeps quiet.'

'Yeah—but will he? You can hear a rider comin' a long way in this stillness, even after dark.'

'He'll keep quiet all right,' said the sheriff. 'When it gets dark we'll gag and tie him.'

This appeared to satisfy Dallas Benton, who raised his glance and turned it westward again for another survey of the sun. For a long time nothing more was said; in fact, except for the faint music of rein-chains, spur rowels, and the gentle rub of leather, the desert around and about was totally hushed. Shadows appeared, long and narrow at first, then widening gradually as the sun sank ever lower, turning a misty, ominous shade of red.

A swift-fox trotting along with its tongue lolling evidently intent upon its own thoughts, came out of the brush ahead, went instantly rigid at sight of the plodding horsemen, then gave a great bound and lit running, its bushy, over-sized tail up like a banner. Farther along they sighted a torpid rattler watching them from fierce and lidless eyes. His body-pattern was interspersed at intervals with outlined lumps where he lay in the meagre shade of a spindly sumac bush.

'Found himself a nest of baby mice,' opined Conley, referring to the lumps. 'Got enough food in him now to last a couple of weeks.' He looked over at Dallas, considering the younger man's condition and also thinking that life, reduced as it now was for all three of them, revolved around such otherwise insignificant things as a torpid rattler full of baby mice.

'Yeah,' mumbled Benton, gazing at the snake as he passed it by.

The reptile did not rattle but kept his fierce and intent eyes upon their every movement, following them on past.

'He could move if he had to,' said Dallas.

Conley twisted for a last look over his shoulder. 'I never kill them unless I have to,' he said. Then faced forward again, his grating eyes moving ahead to Cassady's drooping shoulders. 'After so many years of dealing with men like our friend here, I've gotten so I kind of respect rattlesnakes. They give warning— the Cassadys of this world never do.'

Dallas plodded along, eyes hanging half-closed, lips cracked and swollen, face beet-red, as much from being physically over-heated as from the rays of a sun which he'd circumvented as much as he could by tilting down his hatbrim.

'Someday,' said Dallas Benton eventually, his voice croaking the words and his eyes fixed ahead on something far, far beyond the reach of his vision, 'I'm going to find a land where in summertime it doesn't stay as hot after sundown as it is during sunup. A place where a man can hear water running close by all year round and where there aren't any Jeb Plummers or Burl Cassadys.'

He swung his head. 'You know of such a place, Sheriff?'

'Sure,' murmured Conley.

'Where is it?'

'Someday maybe you'll see it, Dallas. It's a place called heaven.'

Benton forced a wan small smile at Conley. He said no more and kept on riding. Beside him the sheriff spat cotton to clear his mouth-lining of grit, and considered making a cigarette. He didn't do it, though, and after a little more time had passed he tried closing out the world they were shuffling through by lowering his lids.

It didn't work; the heat came into him through his nose and mouth; it lay as a solid weight against each square inch of his skin. He opened his eyes again, looked ahead to Burl Cassady, and said aside to Dallas: 'You suppose the feller who got the idea of Purgatory came from south Texas?'

'No doubt about it,' came Benton's grave response.

They both smiled at this weak joke, feeling their cheeks crack with the effort.

Later, when the sun was finally balanced upon the distant curve of earth, gigantically red and glowing, Conley called another halt. This time he'd selected their resting site with great care, for evening shadows were pooling around them and an acrid coolness was settling. Here they would have a long rest.

As before Conley cared for the horses. He was alert to their every change for without them no matter how wily a man was, how learned in the ways of desert survival, without them there would be no hope at all.

Around them the earth sighed, giving up endless waves of stored heat; the covert, which had hung patiently drooping during the daylight, began its customary recovery. You could infallibly tell when you were approaching the edges of a desert for there were always birds. Here, there were no birds, and Conley reflected that they had still a considerable distance to go.

Be a hell of a note, he told himself when distances blurred and swam in his vision, if he gave out now. Cassady would get away, Plummer would hit Sunflower, Dallas would probably be overtaken and shot by the outlaws, and everything he's suffered so to achieve would count for nothing.

He would never again set eyes on Rose Bell either.

This brought up a sluggishly renewed interest in life and Conley inwardly smiled at himself. A man remained for as long as breath remained, a male animal. What determination alone could not accomplish an appeal to his basic instincts could accomplish. He held to his thoughts of Rose Bell.

The heat continued bad but at least those scalding direct rays were gone. Conley remained over by the animals for a long time, leaning there remembering his last slow-pacing walk with Rose Bell; remembering the highlights of their talk; recalling with no effort at all that moment when she'd raised up on her tiptoes to solidly plant a kiss upon his mouth.

A woman was good for a man. Even her memory was good. Somewhere in the distant past someone had said to Conley that if a man didn't marry before he was thirty years old the chances were excellent that he'd never marry at all.

He dwelt upon this at some length, coming at last to a private conclusion: When a man never married it was more because he'd never felt the pull of a woman singing out to him in a bad hour, than because he'd become habitually accustomed to doing without a woman. Conley could feel Rose Bell's powerful influence sustaining him now. He pushed upright saying to himself that he'd make it all right. He'd make it because she was sending him the strength and the will to make it. Then he went over to the others and sank down there.

CHAPTER NINE

'Divide it up,' said Conley, handing over the canteen to Dallas Benton. 'Judge what you drink by weight.'

Dallas drank, hefted the canteen, took one last swallow and returned the canteen to Conley. The sheriff took two long, slow swallows, and held the canteen away from his face.

'You pretty dry?' he asked Cassady. The outlaw called Conley a vicious name and glared. Conley ignored both the name and the look of savage hate; there was a speculative expression upon his face. He lowered the canteen to his lap and held it there. 'Not too dry to answer a couple of questions, I hope.'

'Damn you,' ground out the renegade. 'If you didn't have that stinkin' canteen you wouldn't get a word out of me!'

'But I do have it, so tell me. Cassady: How did Plummer know there was bullion on that stage?'

'Kid Reilly heard about it up in Alamo City. He cut out for Nacori and told us.'

'How did Plummer know there was enough in the Sunflower bank to make a raid worthwhile?'

'I made that trip myself,' explained the outlaw. 'Rode in and cashed a couple of big bills at the bank an' got the clerk into a conversation. After that, I went down to the liverybarn where those old gaffers sit around all day whittlin', and just listened. I learned all I had to know.'

'Was that Jeb's idea—havin' both places on his schedule for the same day—then plannin' the escape southward in the night?'

'Sure. Who else you figure does the plannin' for our crew?'

Conley did not reply to this, but said instead, 'One thing more, Cassady. Who is Rose Bell?'

At the mention of this name Cassady's eyes swept upwards and slightly widened. For a space of time he said nothing, then, with dawning understanding, he said, 'So that's who it was.'

Dallas Benton, aware that something was

passing between the sheriff and Burl Cassady, now asked, with a puzzled look, 'What was? What's he talkin' about, Sheriff?'

Conley kept his gaze upon the outlaw, waiting, but Cassady, eyes riveted to the lawman's countenance, said nothing. 'Go on,' said the lawman softly. 'Tell him.'

'Dammit,' snapped Benton. 'Tell me what?'

Cassady extended his hand. 'The water,' he said, and for the first time that day he did not sound desperate for it. Conley handed across the canteen, and it was now his turn to smile.

'Drink it all,' he said to Cassady. 'I think we understand each other.'

Over the canteen's spout Cassady's knowing stare clung to Conley's face. He understood perfectly what the sheriff had just done to him. Conley had proved that, although the water was now gone and he could no longer use it as a hold over Cassady, the shooting of Elizabeth Hardin was still their private secret. Cassady had heard Dallas Benton say enough when they had first struck out into the desert, to know who Benton was and why he'd initially gone south to Nacori. All Conley had to do was explain who it was that had shot Elizabeth, then turn his back upon Dallas Benton, and Burl Cassady would be shot to death, gun or no gun, in a twinkling.

Cassady lowered the emptied canteen, turned it upside down so they could all three see that no water remained in it, then he cast

98

the canteen aside. He still did not look from Conley as his tongue made a darting circuit of his lips.

'How about some tobacco?' he asked. Conley passed across the little sack as Dallas Benton muttered a mild curse.

'You two playing some kind of a game, or something?' Benton lay back upon the cooling ground. 'Go ahead and play it—just let me get a little rest.'

Conley watched Cassady twist up the cigarette, retrieved his tobacco and made one himself. He did not offer to hold the light for Cassady, but after igniting his own quirley he said through exhaled smoke, 'I asked you a question about Rose Bell, Cassady.'

'I know you did. I also got something else figured, too.'

'Such as?'

'That damned picture she had of the Plummer gang.'

Conley inclined his head without speaking. Cassady noting this, said next, 'That's how you identified me, isn't it?'

Conley made another slow nod. Cassady, hearing snoring, considered Dallas Benton over a long and speculative moment of thought, then, in a lowered tone, he said, 'The girl didn't die?'

'No she didn't.'

'And she saw the picture too?'

'Yes. She pointed you out as the man who—'

'All right. All right. He may not be asleep,' said Cassady hastily, looking swiftly back at Benton again. 'What about Rose; is she up in Sunflower?'

'Yes.' said Conley. 'She's there.'

To this Cassady said, 'I hope the Kid or Buck see her.' His tone as well as his meaning was bleakly clear.

'You'd better hope just the opposite, Cassady,' stated Conley softly. 'Because if she's been hurt when we get back I promise you this: you won't live to hang.'

Very gradually the outlaw's expression changed. He had seen something in Tim Conley's expression which had caused this to happen. For a time he smoked without speaking, then he regarded his cigarette's ragged tip critically as he said, 'She's married, Conley. Did you know that?'

Conley hadn't known it, and Cassady's calm statement had a solid ring of truthfulness about it. The sheriff's gaze held to Cassady's face over a moment of speechlessness.

'I can see she forgot to tell you that, Sheriff. That's too bad. Maybe you'd like to know who her husband is?'

Conley's reply was barely audible. 'Not you, Cassady?'

'Yes me.'

Conley smoked without saying another word until his cigarette was finished. He plunged it against the soil and sat there

100

regarding its last sputtering little wisps of smoke, then looked up again.

'That explains a lot of things, I reckon,' he exclaimed in an inflectionless voice. 'I can understand how she feels better now—knowing this.'

Cassady made a cold, little smile. 'What you think don't matter, Sheriff. What matters is that she's married and she ain't goin' to get no divorce either, so forget her. She's my property and I don't give up things that belong to me. You remember that, lawman.'

Cassady cocked his head a little to one side. He was slowly coming to consider Sheriff Conley in a new light. As he killed his own cigarette he drawled, 'Course; I just might give her up, Sheriff. An old horse trader like me sort of enjoys makin' trades.'

Conley sighed. In his gentle voice he called Burl Cassady a name no man could overlook. But Cassady overlooked it; he smiled; his slate-coloured eyes gleamed with satisfaction. He had inadvertently struck a soft spot in this hard-eyed, soft spoken lawman.

'Benton's asleep, Sheriff. All you got to do is play like you're also asleep. Who could ever hold it against you? We're all three about ready to drop. You an' Benton just couldn't stay awake any longer—and I escaped. For that little favour I'll just drop plumb out of Rose Bell's life.'

'You'll drop out all right,' retorted Conley.

101

'Through the trapdoor of a scaffold.'

Cassady was undismayed; too many things were beginning to add up in his favour. He shrugged. 'Have it your way then. But you'll never have her. Never in God's green world, Sheriff, because I'm not going to hang. You'll see.'

Conley stood up and stretched. Around them now, swift desert dusk was descending. He crossed to the side of Dallas Benton and roughly prodded the younger man with his toe. Benton opened one red-rimmed and swollen eye. 'Get up,' said the sheriff. 'Let's go.'

Benton sat up, peered wetly around, then arose to spank away cloying dust and sand. He afterwards crossed to the horses and there, seeing Cassady fumbling with his chincha, Dallas said to the sheriff, 'How about gagging him?'

'Good idea,' murmured Conley without looking around. 'Take care of it, Dallas.'

Cassady turned with a quick scowl and a protest. Neither the lawman nor Dallas Benton heeded him. Dallas instead of using either his or the sheriff's handkerchief for the gag, gravely tugged the outlaw's shirt loose from the waist, tore off a goodly portion of the lower half and made a gag. When he was ready to apply this, Cassady began to rant and curse.

Benton looked over at Conley. 'You want to give me a hand here?' he asked.

Conley rose up and settled across his saddle.

From this eminence he said quietly, 'Shoot him. We can't waste a lot of time messing around with the likes of him. Just shoot him an' we won't have to bother with the gag.'

Cassady, hearing these words and seeing in Tom Conley's face a dispassionate hardness, said not another word and offered himself willingly for the gagging. Dallas Benton laughed at this abrupt change, gagged the outlaw then got astride and eased out beside the sheriff. 'That scairt hell out of him,' he said, turning to look at Conley.

Conley nodded, watching Cassady riding along, but he said nothing, and Benton's twinkling eyes gradually lost their look of amusement. 'By God,' he said in a tone that was close to awe. 'You meant that, didn't you?'

Still Conley said nothing.

There rose up around them now, an almost audible sighing of parched earth. The heat was still there, punishingly fierce, but without the sun's savage glare it was at least bearable. Their horses, badly tucked-up and shuffling along head-hung and listless, were not too far from the failing point. This occupied Conley for the better part of that long evening. He favoured the animals as much as he could, and after full dark, although it was against his better judgment, he angled slightly to the east. Burl Cassady did not appear to notice this; he was poking along as head-hung as his mount. But Dallas Benton noticed the slight variation in their course and queried Conley about it. The sheriff's reply was terse.

'This is a big country, boy. Forsythe and Reilly will naturally take the shortest route southward towards their rendezvous with Plummer. I'm hoping to miss them by deviating a little from the bee-line trail to Sunflower.'

Benton was satisfied and said no more.

More time passed; it seemed to Tim Conley that he had been in the saddle throughout an eternity. His body was dry to the point of agony, his joints worked grittily and his mind seemed only occasionally to obey his will. From time to time his vision grew fuzzy. He had had less water than either Benton or his prisoner and this was beginning to sap him.

He had, from the outset at Nacori, sought at his own expense to alleviate so far as possible the anguish of his companions. He wanted particularly to get them back to Sunflower rational and alive. To achieve this he'd decided to sacrifice his share of the drinking water in order that they might make it through. He had also known that he was physically tougher than either Dallas or Cassady; he'd banked on this, had gone on drawing upon his own physical reserves for as long as he could.

Part of the mechanism he had employed to keep from thinking of his own weakening state had been to think of other people; of Rose Bell and eventually of Elizabeth.

He felt almost certain by this time that Elizabeth had died. He could not explain to himself why he was so positive about this; he had known a number of people with lung-shot-wounds who had survived handily. It never did occur to him that this morbidity might be a reflection of his own mental depression.

And Rose Bell . . . She had no friends in Sunflower; in fact had no place to live, except at Joel Hardin's home. But Joel Hardin was a kindly man. A little flighty at times, as he'd been that afternoon Conley had returned with the posse after his initial search for the man who had shot Elizabeth.

Joel would look out for Rose Bell.

Conley's mind closed down around that name. He'd thought it was both her first and last names and that was ironic because both those names were her given names. Actually she was Rose Bell Cassady.

That night when she'd given him the picture, he thought now, she had known he was going after her husband. No wonder she'd turned away from him, had silently cried there by the late-blooming paloverde tree and had afterwards been short with him. She'd thought he meant to kill her husband—and she had been right, thought Cassady. If things had worked out differently he would have killed him. Might kill him yet despite the fact that, knowing Cassady as well as he now did, he viewed him with more contempt than hatred.

You had to about half respect a man to want to kill him; when all you felt was deep scorn the idea of killing seemed beneath you, seemed contemptible.

It had been an ordeal for Rose Bell. More of an ordeal than he had thought that night by the paloverde tree, and he had thought then she was suffering agonies. She had said she had never before wanted another human being hurt; that she wasn't certain *what* she wanted for the man who had shot down Elizabeth Hardin.

Of course she hadn't been certain. There was something Conley had learned about women through years of observation in his trade; hating men as badly as some women did; wishing momentarily for as much agony to be vented against them as it was possible for a woman to wish for, they nevertheless never quite rid themselves of memories of other times with the men they hated, and in the end, usually tearfully, they rescinded their wished-for calamities.

This, he thought, had been Rose Bell's state of mind that night when she and Conley had last talked together. Despite her anguish and terrible memories of life with Burl Cassady, she could remember other days and probably other nights with him. She could wish he'd be punished for what he'd done, but in the end she'd actually only wish for him to be removed forever from her life.

Why hadn't she told him Cassady was her husband?

Because she had considered it likely that Conley would take chances in order not to have to kill him? Perhaps. Possibly too, for a searing hot moment she had hoped Conley *would* kill Cassady.

There could be a dozen explanations, thought Conley, and very likely he would never know which, actually, was the right one. One thing he knew of a certainty: if Rose Bell did not voluntarily tell him, he would never ask her.

Dallas Benton's voice, sharp-pitched, caught Conley's attention, freeing him from his reverie by its quick sound of alarm.

'Sheriff; I think I hear a horse coming. Maybe two horses.'

Something icy touched down through Conley clearing his mind in an instant. He straightened instinctively in the saddle drawing forward to listen. On ahead Burl Cassady went unheedingly plodding along.

'Stop him,' said Conley sharply to Dallas Benton. 'You two keep quiet.'

Moments later he heard the first sound. It was made by one rider, not two. This horseman was sweeping along southerly directly towards them in a loose gallop. A knife-edged warning flashed along Conley's nerves, alerting every fibre of his being to fresh peril. Where, he wanted to know, was the second outlaw?

Behind him Dallas called softly: 'He's making straight for us. It's too late to avoid him.'

Conley was irritated by this call and threw an angry look at young Benton. If they could hear the approaching rider so also could he hear them.

The horseman was coming on at a steady pace and Conley, deciding the man had enough of his own noise to contend with, knew he had not heard Dallas's call because the man neither stopped nor made any swerving attempt to conceal his presence in the night.

Conley then started forward to intercept the stranger. It was beginning to occur to him that this might not be either Reilly or Forsythe at all. They would be riding together; Burl Cassady had said as much.

Whether it was or not Conley had the advantage; he knew someone was approaching him while the oncoming rider did not apparently have any idea he was being stalked by the sheriff of Sunflower.

Surprise was always a good element, particularly when a man was engaged in the work of law enforcement. Conley had always valued it highly; felt now a little sense of elation because he had it now.

His fuzziness of mind dropped entirely away. From some secret well-spring within him had come at this crucial moment the infusion of energy he needed. He entirely forgot the spreading numbness and dehydration of his body as he moved forward stealthily in the velvet gloom.

CHAPTER TEN

Conley was wrong; the moving silhouette was indeed one of Plummer's gang, but before he had ascertained this for himself there came a quick shout behind and west of him, then a gunshot.

Instantly the man Conley was approaching spun away, went down over his animal's neck and flung backwards a random shot. It was a blur of moves in blinding sequence. Conley, going for his own gun after that shot, heard the outlaw's bullet sing past. Then he also fired, but his shot was far too hasty and behind him came a third shot, this one, he thought, made by the gun of Dallas Benton.

Conley knew, even as he spun back towards Benton and Burl Cassady, what had happened. The two outlaws were riding perhaps a hundred yards apart, and the man farthest west had stumbled upon Dallas and their prisoner. He had probably not recognised either of them, but a wanted man, encountering waiting strangers in the pit of night, did not hold his fire; he shot first and investigated later.

Dallas was afoot and Burl Cassady, wide awake now and flattened upon the ground, was straining to call out around his gag. Conley, approaching him from the rear, looked down for a moment, then dispassionately swung his hand-gun in a heavy arc. Dallas Benton swung around at the sound of metal crunching against bone, then speared a quick upward look at the sheriff.

'Just put him to sleep,' said Conley, turning slightly away from Cassady's slumped and death-like stillness. 'Where is the one that shot at you?'

Benton returned his attention to the night around them. 'Out there somewhere,' he said vaguely, indicating a westerly direction with his gunbarrel. 'What the hell happened?'

'They weren't together. While I was watching the one we heard, the other one came down beside you saw you and fired.'

'Which is which?' Benton asked.

Conley grunted. 'It makes no difference,' he said, kneeling, the better to skyline this land which had suddenly filled up with lethal perils.

Benton came close to say, 'They didn't run for it. I haven't heard any horses running behind us.'

'No,' said Conley, probing the night. 'And I don't think they will either.' He was thinking that Reilly and Buck Forsythe would have to determine who they were, and either eliminate

110

them or capture them, before Jeb Plummer and the others came up.

'Sure quiet out there,' said Benton, shucking his spent cartridge and plugging in a fresh load. 'What d'we do now?'

'Wait—and be quiet.'

They waited.

Overhead was a clear, crystal wash of stars and a thin moon hanging steady and smoke-yellow in the sky. Ordinarily there would have been coyotes tonguing, or little swift-foxes yap-yap-yapping; maybe even a cougar screaming or little desert wrens chuckering sleepily in the underbrush. Now, there was none of this, for if man-smell had not frightened away all wildlife, then those shots had.

Conley wished he dared make a cigarette. Beside him, evidently Benton was wishing something similar, for he raised up, threw a raking look outward and around, then muttered something under his breath and lay flat again.

Out of the east came a flat call, laying its echo harshly over the darkness. 'Hey; you fellers over there: Who are you?'

Conley signalled for Benton to keep quiet. Neither of them moved nor answered. After a time the same voice called forth again, this time though from a different position, and that made Conley smile; these were no novices, these two night-riders of Jeb Plummer's.

'Listen; identify yourselves and chances are

we'll ride on. Who the hell are you?'

Still Conley and Dallas Benton said nothing. Now, from west, and a little south of them, came another voice, harsher sounding.

'You want to play hide'n seek it's all right with us,' this outlaw yelled. 'Only this ain't no game and you'll likely wind up bein' buzzard bait.'

Conley bent low saying to Dallas Benton, 'That one's pretty long-winded. The next time he speaks peg his position while he's talkin' and let him have one.'

Dallas nodded. Beside them Burl Cassady groaned around his gag. In the utter stillness this sound carried. Almost at once the man to the east called to his pardner.

'Kid; they might be downed. I heard someone groan just now.'

To this Kid Reilly made a cynical reply. 'Go take a look. I'll wait right where I am.'

For a time there was silence again, then Conley, watching the east, thought he sighted faint movement. He lay a hand lightly upon Dallas Benton's shoulder warning him with this pressure not to move. Dallas understood and obeyed. Conley pressed lower upon the ground staring at the horizon with half-closed eyes, as though testing the dead night air; he sighted that blur of movement again. It was a man and it was coming on from a crouched position, as though the man were down on all fours. Now and then the man would halt, fade out in murk and remain like that, motionless, listening, for a time, then he would start forward again.

Conley spared a quick look at Dallas Benton. The younger man was holding to his vigil westward; his gunhand was pushed forward, waiting. Conley now raised up just the slightest bit and with infinite caution, to get both feet set hard against the ground; he meant to fire, if he had to, then spring away before muzzleblast drew a bullet towards him. His body was tensed.

Ahead, that indistinct blur came on. Then, close enough for Conley to get a fairly good look at the man—as good a look as the meagre light permitted—the outlaw stopped again. This time he seemed to sense trouble, for he hung there on all fours without moving, then very gently settled flat upon the ground.

Conley wondered if the renegade had silhouetted him; if he had it couldn't be helped; Conley dared not move now or the man would see him easily. He hung there, lizard-like, suspended slightly off the ground with his legs aching from this unaccustomed position.

Behind him Burl Cassady stirred and groaned again.

The outlaw, evidently drawing assurance from this, raised up and moved forward once again. He seemed now to be abandoning some of his extreme caution. Conley flexed his legs slightly, waiting. The outlaw came straight onward and when he was less than fifty feet away Conley sucked back a very gradual, deep breath. It occurred to him that, with luck, he might not have to shoot this man at all. Unless the renegade deviated from his course he would come right up to Conley.

Out of the west came a sharp call. Kid Reilly was impatient, or uneasy, or both; his voice was garrulous now. 'Hey, Buck; you gone to sleep over there?'

Forsythe's head jerked at the sound of his pardner's voice but he made no reply. He did, though, begin his forward crawl again, and more swiftly now, as though impelled forward by Reilly's impatience.

Conley measured the distance which was closing between them. Forty feet, thirty feet, twenty feet; then Forsythe halted, and this time Conley could see his body stiffening. Either Forsythe had seen Benton or Cassady move behind Conley, or else he had received some intuitive warning about continuing. In either case, Conley knew he could expect his prey to come no closer. He dug in his toes and moved.

Buck Forsythe, momentarily stunned by the flying shape hurtling overhand towards him, whirled up off the ground in one wild leap. Then Conley's body struck him and he let off a fierce burst of breath and went over backwards, his pistol knocked violently from his grasp.

Conley felt the scrabbling hands tearing at him. He raised his gun-hand and let it fall. Forsythe, however, was arching, writhing, twisting and wrenching to get free and the gun struck hard upon the ground. Conley tried again, and again the frantic man beneath him pulled away at the last moment. Now Conley let go the gun and went to work with his fists. He could not at once strike any telling blows because Forsythe's squirming kept him from getting poised. Then, catching the renegade's throat, Conley levered himself partially upright and swung. At the same moment behind him a gun exploded. There was one shot, a pause, then two more explosions almost atop one another. Finally, there was one last shot, then stillness. Conley, feeling Forsythe go limp under him, twisted for a rearward glance. Dallas Benton was rising up.

'Down,' said Conley. 'Get down, damn you!'

Dallas Benton dropped as though Conley's words had clubbed him to earth. He turned so that he could look back. His pale face was sweat-shiny in the starshine.

Conley returned his attention to Buck Forsythe, who was not moving. He then retrieved his pistol, flung away Forsythe's weapon, and lay back to draw in several great breaths of the hot night air.

'I got him,' said Dallas Benton now, his

voice full of confidence and protest. 'I saw him rise up and go over backwards. I got him all right.'

Conley raised up and shook himself. 'Watch this one,' he ordered, and started forward westerly.

Dallas had been correct. Kid Reilly lay at the base of a wiry, ancient chaparral bush. He had two bullets in him and he was very dead. Conley knelt, rolled Reilly face up, peered closely at his face, then arose nodding. Rose Bell's identification of this outlaw in the photograph tallied with the man at his feet. He returned to Dallas.

'You sure hit him,' said Benton, shaking Forsythe. Conley only glanced where Dallas was kneeling, then he faced about where a man was staggering upright. He crossed over, cut the gag and gave Cassady a push. 'Over by your friend there and sit down,' he ordered. 'Dallas?'

'Yeah?'

'Get the horses.'

Benton stood up, he peered at the sheriff as he dusted his knees. 'What about Kid Reilly?'

'You got him with both slugs. Now go get the horses.'

Dallas departed without resentment; he could see how Sheriff Conley was verging on collapse. As soon as the younger man strode off Conley sank down and began curling up a cigarette. Across from him Burl Cassady was beginning to forget his own ills as he made out the still form of Buck Forsythe close by.

'Hey,' he said suddenly, lifting round eyes to Conley. 'He's dead.'

Conley licked the paper, folded it over, rummaged for a match, flicked it alight and deeply inhaled. Then he spoke. 'Kid Reilly is, but Forsythe's only knocked out.'

Cassady bent to peer at the unconscious man. 'What'n hell'd you hit him with?' He asked, straightening up.

'My fist,' said the lawman. 'On you I used a gun-barrel.' Conley smoked a moment, listening to hoof-falls out on the desert. 'You're smarter than I thought, Cassady.'

The outlaw was probing gingerly atop his head where a sullen bump throbbed. He considered Conley balefully but was silent.

'It wasn't any accident those two were combing their way southward. Is that another of Jeb's ideas?'

'Sure. He always made us ride fanned out.'

'It's good strategy,' conceded Conley. 'It damned near got one of 'em past us, too.' Conley exhaled. 'That's the part you didn't tell us, isn't it?'

'Yes.'

Conley sighed. 'Like I said: you're smarter than I thought. You figured we'd hear 'em coming anyway, so you told us they were coming south. Then you deliberately withheld the information that they wouldn't be riding together hoping we'd ride right between them and get it from both sides. Right?'

'Right, Conley,' said Cassady. 'You're good at figurin' things out—after they happen.'

Conley shrugged. 'I'm alive—Reilly isn't.'

Dallas came forward leading four saddle animals. He dropped something metallic and heavy at Conley's feet.

'Two full canteens,' he said. 'Right now they're worth fighting for all by themselves.'

Conley unscrewed one canteen's cap, tilted back his head and drank; let cool water cut the scorch in his throat, run down over inflamed membranes assuaging the agony which had been tormenting him all day and on into this night. He swallowed noisily, slowly, and luxuriantly, then put aside the canteen, took a deep drag off his cigarette and exhaled. He looked over where Dallas was hunkering and smiled. Sweat was bursting out under his shirt again; it shone on his face and even his eyes lost that feverish dryness which had glazed them since early afternoon.

'I needed that more than a million dollars,' he said.

Dallas Benton made a slow, understanding smile at Conley.

CHAPTER ELEVEN

'You need this too,' said the younger man, bending down to kneel near Conley. He was holding in one extended hand two Sonora oranges and a flat can of sardines. Conley took them and began eating. Beside him Dallas Benton considered the two remaining oranges, then tossed one over to Burl Cassady. The renegade, watching Conley eating, said, 'What the hell—how come him to get the sardines.'

'You been drinking his water all day,' growled Benton. 'Eat your orange be grateful.'

Cassady ate the orange but did not appear very grateful.

Later, they lashed Kid Reilly across his horse, tied Buck Forsythe's ankles under the belly of his animal, secured his wrists behind him, and started slowly northward again. It was now late, and there was a blessed coolness to the night.

Conley began feeling better. He drank again, some time later, and so did Dallas Benton. Even Burl Cassady tanked up. This emptied one of the captured canteens but it no longer mattered; they still had a full canteen with them and Sunflower was not more than an hour's ride onward.

Conley turned to consider the country they had passed over. It was in his mind that the

Plummer gang would be hurrying by now, and because they had fresher horses he thought it not improbable that they would not be too far behind. Maybe eight miles, perhaps less; Jeb Plummer was a wily person. If there was a way to make good time he would know it.

Benton, watching Conley's thoughtful face, now said, 'They couldn't have heard those shots, could they?'

'No,' said the sheriff, 'it's hardly likely.'

'Sound carries out here.'

'Not that far though.'

Conley held himself around in the saddle for a little longer. He was considering the immediate future. It would of course be a simple thing to foil Plummer's raid upon the Sunflower bank, but he wanted more than just that. A man who has sweated off ten pounds, gone without rest or relaxation for so many hours, and who has had his life endangered by another man, wishes for more than just escape. He wants vengeance, and Tim Conley was no exception to this rule. Finally, he made a cigarette and rode along lost in thought, smoking, and occasionally raising his head to keen the night around them.

'Forsythe's perking up,' said Benton, after a while.

Conley threw forward a look. Cassady was speaking to the other prisoner; telling him about Kid Reilly and what had happened back in Nacori, and later. Forsythe's back was to

Benton and Conley, but he twisted to gaze around and his stare fell upon the lawman's neutral, considering, features. He said nothing, and ultimately returned his attention to Cassady. In this fashion they continued down the night, the four of them, until, shortly before midnight, Sunflower's orange lights showed ahead low on the horizon. At that welcome vision Conley sighed.

'Made it,' he grunted, not particularly speaking to anyone. But Dallas Benton, heeding these words, also spoke.

'What d'the Mexes say: "*la noche triste*." The sad night?'

'For Kid Reilly, maybe. For us, rough, but not sad.'

'Sheriff?'

Conley looked around.

'Which one shot Elizabeth?'

'You'll know in good time,' said the lawman. 'In good time, Dallas. For now, let's worry about something else.'

'Such as?'

'It's only partly done—this business with Plummer. He's still coming up here, y'know.'

But Dallas Benton had evidently been thinking also, for he now began to slowly wag his head. 'I doubt that, Sheriff. When he doesn't meet Reilly and Forsythe he's not likely to keep on coming.'

'He'll meet Forsythe all right,' said the sheriff, 'and he'll see the man he figures is

Reilly too.'

'Huh? How?'

Conley tilted his head to chin-point towards the nearing few lights of Sunflower. 'Not many folks about,' he said, meaning in the town. 'It's pretty late.'

'What's that got to do with it?'

'Maybe not very much,' conceded Conley. 'But as soon as we ride in you head for the liverybarn. Get us a couple of fresh horses.'

'What'll you be doin'?'

'Lockin' up our friend Cassady and waiting for you.'

That wasn't all Conley had in mind, but it was all he said right then, because they were coming into Sunflower's southern environs. At his side Dallas Benton was riding with a dark scowl. When they came abreast of Conley's jailhouse he said, 'Go on; get the fresh animals,' to Dallas Benton, then swung in at his own hitchrail and got stiffly down. Burl Cassady and Buck Forsythe had to be freed of ropes before they could also dismount. Fading out in the northerly stillness of late night, were the hoof-falls of Dallas Benton's mount.

'Inside,' said Conley to his captives.

He lit a lamp in the jaillhouse, locked Burl Cassady in a cell and left Buck Forsythe's hands tied behind him. He then made coffee on a little iron cook-stove and filled four cups with it. One of these he gave to Cassady through bars, the second cup he held for

122

Forsythe to drink from, while the third and fourth cups he took back to his desk with him, set one of them down and drank the other cup empty in four large gulps. Weariness began almost at once to depart from him. He had not, up until now, said five words to Buck Forsythe.

Fixing his even gaze upon the outlaw he asked: 'What did you find here, in Sunflower?'

'What d'you mean?' countered the renegade.

'Could Plummer take the bank or couldn't he?'

'What difference does that make, now?' growled the bound man.

'Not a bit of difference to you,' said the lawman, 'but a lot of difference to me. You see—I'm going to keep your date with Jeb. I'll want to know what to tell him.'

This caused Forsythe's face to pucker up with puzzlement. After considering Conley for a while he said, doubtingly, 'You're not in with Jeb—are you?'

From behind his cell bars Cassady hooted at Forsythe. 'You idiot—he's our worst enemy.'

Conley threw his gaze cell-ward. 'One more word out of you,' he said to Cassady, 'and I'll unlock that door and let Dallas loose on you for Elizabeth.'

Cassady said no more; he sipped his coffee and listened, but was entirely silent.

'Well . . .?' demanded Conley. 'What were

you going to tell Jeb?'

'It's a push-over.'

'The bank?'

'Yeah.'

'Anything else?'

Forsythe looked puzzled again. 'Like what?' he asked. 'All we were supposed to do was sort of scout-up the place.'

Conley nodded, listening to sounds of horses beyond the door. 'I hope for your sake you're telling me the truth,' he told Forsythe, 'because you're going with us—and if there's any slip-up you'll be the first one to get it.'

Forsythe's puzzled look vanished. He watched Sheriff Conley get tiredly up from his chair and cross to the door, fling it open and say, 'There's a cup of java in here for you, Dallas.'

Benton crossed into the room with a bounding step. His face was filthy, sweat-sticky and beard-stubbled, but his eyes were brightly shining. 'She's better,' he cried out to Conley. 'Elizabeth's better, Sheriff. She's going to make it in fine shape.'

Doubting this, Conley said, 'Where'd you hear that?'

'At the barn. The nighthawk—old Jay Brown—told me. He liked to fainted when I rode in. Said rumour had you'n me dead down in Nacori.'

Conley rubbed his jaw. 'I hope his story about Elizabeth's closer to the truth than that other rumour is.' He watched Dallas cross to his desk, take up the cup of coffee and drain it without stopping. He was thinking of the liverybarn night-man. Jay Brown was a quiet, decent sort of elderly person; he had never known him to knowingly tell an untruth. Conley looked past Forsythe and Benton to find Burl Cassady's gaze strongly upon him. The outlaw's countenance shone with powerful relief.

'Can't hang a man for a near-miss,' he said to Conley.

Over his cup's thick rim Dallas Benton's eyes swept to Cassady's face and clung there. He very gradually lowered the cup. 'You?' He said, then, when Cassady continued to look triumphantly at Conley, ignoring him, Dallas said to the sheriff. 'Him? Did he shoot her?'

Conley nodded, then said, 'Never mind that; we've got other things to do. He'll be here when we get back.'

Benton put the cup down and stood there in the centre of the room, his face darkening with a rush of blood. Burl Cassady, seeing this, moved well back from the front bars of his cell.

'Where are the keys?' asked Benton in a soft tone. 'Sheriff; give me the key to his cell.'

Conley had the key in his pocket. He shook his head saying, 'Later. Like I just told you, boy; he'll be here when we get back. Now fetch Forsythe along and let's get riding.'

'I owe him something, Sheriff. It won't delay

us. Just five minutes is all I ask.'

Conley's eyes hardened against the younger man. His tone roughened when next he spoke. 'Benton; you owe me something too. Now fetch Forsythe and come along!' These words cut sharply through the jailhouse's stillness. Dallas turned finally, without another look at Burl Cassady, crossed over to Forsythe, caught at him and gave him a savage shove.

Outside again, Sheriff Tim Conley carefully locked the massive jailhouse door behind them, watched Benton secure Buck Forsythe to a fresh animal, then crossed over to his own new mount. From the saddle he said, 'I wish I knew how much time we have. I'd like to round up a posse.'

'It's late,' retorted Benton from his position in the saddle beside Buck Forsythe. 'By the time we could roust up some of the boys, get 'em saddled up and ready, it'd be a heap later.'

This was what Conley had already considered, so he lifted his reins, wheeled away from the hitchrack and struck out southward saying nothing more until they had cleared Sunflower. Then he twisted to cast a speculative look at their prisoner.

'You better be good at play-acting,' he told Forsythe. His meaning was clear enough. Forsythe rode along with a grim and uncomfortable look upon his face, not deigning to reply.

It was well past midnight. Behind them

126

nearly all the lights were out, now, in Sunflower. Overhead a yeasty flashing of starshine filled the universe, and the smoke-yellow moon was rapidly falling away.

Conley's mount proved to be a sensible, plodding beast, full of rest and tamed-down wickedness. He would, from time to time, like most wise livery animals, try occasionally to edge around and head back for home. But this did not annoy the sheriff, as it would have at some other time. He was almost grateful for the occupation which kept him alert, for he was by this time, despite the black coffee, bone-weary. He thought wryly that if he had not eaten the oranges and the sardines, had not had his fill of water, the agony would have kept him at least awake. Now, this was no longer the case and he plodded along, watching the horse, drowsily considering what he must do before this night was done. Except for that coffee he'd drunk he'd have fallen asleep in the saddle.

CHAPTER TWELVE

They had travelled three miles back down into the desert before any of them spoke, then it was Buck Forsythe, and his words implied considerable thought since leaving Sunflower.

'Listen, Sheriff,' he said earnestly to Tim

Conley, 'if you're figurin' on using me for bait you're makin' a wrong guess about Jeb. He won't fall for it.'

'Maybe,' grunted Conley, his attention elsewhere.

'Dammit, Sheriff, I *know* Jeb.'

Conley turned now to gaze upon his prisoner. Forsythe's face was shiny with fresh perspiration and his eyes were nervously plumbing the night ahead. 'It'll be up to you,' said Conley. 'Entirely up to you, Buck.'

'What do you mean?'

'Well,' said the lawman, 'I think we'd better stop about where we are.' He looked over at Dallas Benton nodding. Dallas reined up, drawing Forsythe's animal also to a halt. 'Now get down,' ordered the sheriff. Dallas swung off and roughly assisted Forsythe from the saddle. 'Now sit down and relax,' said Conley, still using his dispassionate, impersonal tone. 'Here; make a smoke for him, Dallas.' Conley passed over the papers and sack of tobacco. Throughout all this Forsythe's moving glance kept returning to the sheriff. He very obviously wanted to say something, but he did not. The restraint made his lips a thin line.

'Now,' said Conley, watching Dallas work, 'we'll just wait and listen.'

Dallas popped the cigarette into Forsythe's mouth and held the match. Forsythe took a deep drag and exhaled. He said, 'There'll be four of them, Sheriff, at least. Even if you're

128

lucky and get one or two, you'll play hell getting Jeb and at least one other. You know that, don't you?'

Conley took back the makings and began manufacturing a cigarette of his own. 'It'll help to even the odds,' he said. 'But I'm hoping to take all four of them—and alive.' He lit up, removed the cigarette and gazed upon Forsythe. 'You're going to talk to them, Buck. You're going to tell Jeb in your own way exactly what you'd have told him if we hadn't captured you.'

'Yeah? And what do I tell him about Kid Reilly?'

'That his horse went lame and that he's waiting back in town.'

Buck Forsythe considered this, then began wagging his head. 'I don't think Jeb'll believe it. You see; when any of us are sent out in pairs, we're supposed to return the same way.'

'Anyone could have a horse go lame on them,' contributed Dallas Benton.

Forsythe looked at Dallas. 'You're pretty young,' he said, as though this excused Dallas for making some kind of idiotic remark. To Conley he directed a longer address. 'Sheriff; you don't know Jeb. If the sun goes behind a cloud he's suspicious. If someone's late to a rendezvous, he's waiting with a gun. If I show up without Kid Reilly he won't believe the Kid's critter lamed-up on him.'

'What will he think?'

129

'That me bein' alone is some kind of a trap.'

Again Dallas spoke up. 'How the hell would he think Kid Reilly could keep up with you if he was afoot?'

Once more Forsythe bent upon Dallas Benton his look of irascibility. 'Look, boy,' he ground out. 'You don't put a man like Kid Reilly on foot—lame horse or no damned lame horse. Do you understand?'

'No,' said Dallas frankly, 'I don't.'

'Reilly would have stolen a horse from one of those hitchrails in town. If my hands were free, kid, I'd make you a sand-drawing.'

Again Forsythe turned away from Benton to frown at the sheriff. 'It won't work,' he said. 'All's going to happen is a gunfight with me out in front and unarmed—tied up like a goddamned turkey.'

'Possibly,' agreed Conley. 'That's another reason why I brought you along, Buck. You'll get it first. I told you that back at the jailhouse.'

Forsythe's sweating countenance was facing fully towards the lawman. He was seeking to determine in his own mind whether Tim Conley was actually this impersonally deadly or not. He licked his lips thinking that Conley *was* that heartless. On his face now, showed fresh, raw fear.

'On the other hand,' went on Conley, 'you know Jeb. If there's a way to save your hide and help me get him, you'd better come up with it.' Conley cocked his head, lowered his voice and finished with: 'And you'd better be quick about it too.'

Forsythe, and also Dallas Benton, straightened up to also plumb the night southward for sounds. They detected none. For that matter neither had Tim Conley, but his purpose had been effectively accomplished; Forsythe's paling face glistened.

'Shoot first,' he said. 'That's the only thing to do. As soon as you can make 'em out, Sheriff, open up on 'em. There isn't any other way.'

To this Dallas Benton growled, 'I hope I never have as good a friend as you are to Plummer.'

Conley let this pass without comment. He punched out his cigarette in the dirt and for a long time said no more. Then, slanting a narrowed gaze over at Forsythe he spoke again.

'You can stop them by calling out, Buck. Afterwards you'd better go down and lie still.'

Forsythe nodded glumly; he'd already made up his mind to do this. In fact he'd made up his mind to something else, too, on the long ride from Sunflower. It was better to be alive in a prison than dead in the middle of a sun-blasted desert. He would sell out Jeb Plummer or anyone else, for that matter, in order to remain alive. He now said, 'Sheriff; they won't come at you all in a group.'

'No,' agreed Conley. 'I sort of had a notion about that from the way you and Reilly met us. What does Plummer use—a kind of vidette screen, like they use in the army?'

'Yes. There'll be one rider far out ahead like a scout. There'll be two others east and west maybe a couple hundred yards.'

Dallas Benton began to wryly wag his head. He murmured: 'No wonder Plummer's usually so successful.'

Neither Forsythe nor Tim Conley paid him any attention; their gazes were locked across the small interval which separated them.

'Thanks,' said Conley, in a tone as dry as old corn husks. 'Anything else?'

'One more thing. I'll help you in return for your help later on—if your scheme to catch Jeb comes off, and if I'm tried.'

'I can say that you helped, Forsythe. That's all.' Conley cocked his head to listen again; the night continued deathly still. He straightened again, saying, 'If I were you though, I wouldn't try anything heroic, because if Plummer doesn't get you I will.'

'I'll keep out of it.'

Dallas killed his cigarette and spat aside. 'You should; you win no matter which side loses.'

Forsythe turned on the younger man an ironic expression. 'You've got a lot of years yet to live, kid,' he said. 'No one likes selling out their friends—but life is something you don't want to be in any hurry to move out of, either.' He paused, then added. 'You'll find out about those things, someday.'

Dallas gazed over at Conley. 'You goin' to leave him tied?'

'Of course,' answered the lawman. Then he made a very small and mirthless grin at Forsythe. 'If I lose and Jeb finds you tied, it'll help.'

Forsythe looked as though he might say thank you, but he didn't. He only spat out the cigarette and fixed upon it his bitter gaze.

Conley arose silently, stood a moment listening, then said to Dallas, 'Keep an eye on him,' and moved off towards their horses. These, he took back a long hundred yards and tied, then returned to where Forsythe and Dallas Benton sat cross-legged in deep silence, paused for only a brief glance downward, then continued on southward for a way into the desert.

There was the continuing hush all around Conley as he paced steadily along for perhaps a quarter mile before stopping. It occurred to him that perhaps Jeb Plummer might not come north after all; that because he was so wily, the absence of Burl Cassady might make him suspicious. And, the longer Conley stood there in the cool darkness, the more he almost came to wish this might be the case. He was now no longer driven by his earlier wish to make Plummer's gang of renegades pay for the

133

shooting of Elizabeth Hardin. For his own perils and discomfort, he was prepared to shrug them off as part of the duties of office. He made a cigarette, lit it behind his shielding hatbrim, and smoked it behind a cupped hand.

There was of course the matter of Plummer's many other depredations to be remembered. Also, there was Conley's conviction that this particular band of outlaws had to be stopped, and finally, there was the anguish, the suffering and the degradation brought to others—to Rose Bell Cassady for instance. Conley sucked back a big lungful of smoke, dropped and ground out the cigarette, then exhaled. No, he told himself, he did not actually wish Plummer would not come up out of the desert at all; he simply wished that he, himself, felt less weary so that when they met he'd be able to concentrate on that meeting.

Southward, so faint at first as to be scarcely heard at all, was the soft music of rein-chains. Conley shook his head, then became absolutely motionless, listening. Sometimes, he thought, when a man has endured too much and his body is past the point of exhaustion, he can imagine things.

Then the sound came again; this time accompanied by the sharp, metallic scuff of a horseshoe striking granite. Conley waited no longer, but faced about and hastened back to where Dallas Benton still squatted across from head-hung and motionless Buck Forsythe.

Dallas uncoiled up off the ground as Conley approached, seeing in the older man's purposeful stride a reason for an ending of this long waiting.

'You hear 'em?' he breathlessly asked.

'Yes. Still about half a mile off.' Dallas Benton's lethargy fell away in a twinkling. Conley saw this and was reassured by it. He looked past to Buck Forsythe, saying to the outlaw, 'On your feet.' The renegade awkwardly arose.

'You'll hear them soon now,' said the sheriff. 'And Buck—your life depends upon how you act.'

Forsythe heard without speaking. His face was pinched down with apprehension. His eyes rummaged the southerly night, constantly moving. Finally, as both Dallas Benton and Tim Conley palmed their six-guns, Forsythe spoke to the sheriff.

'I don't think this'll work,' he said swiftly. 'You'd better drop back to Sunflower. At least up there you can get help when the fight starts.'

'All you have to worry about,' rejoined the lawman, 'is your part in stopping them.'

Dallas Benton, too, was struck by last-minute misgivings. He started to voice them, but Sheriff Conley, after listening to only the initial words, cut across Benton's voice with words of his own.

'Listen, boy; if it's much of a fight the sound

of it will carry back to Sunflower. Don't worry—if they dismount we can hold them until help arrives.'

'And if they stay in the saddle . . .?'

'The worst we'll do then,' answered Conley, 'is scatter them to the four winds.'

'Still, I wish we'd taken the time to round up a posse.'

'Did you know we'd have this much time?' challenged the sheriff. Dallas shook his head, beginning to hear sounds out over the dark desert. 'Neither did I,' Conley said to him, 'so we'll do the best we can and hope for the best. In my experience, Dallas, when a man gives everything he's got, it's usually just about enough.'

Benton's youthful face tightened up; his jaw got hard-set in a way that reassured the sheriff, and he nodded. 'All right,' he said in a low tone. 'Let 'em come.'

Forsythe was standing very erectly now, also listening. After a time his voice came into the stillness very softly. 'It's them all right; I recognise the way they're riding.'

'Where will Plummer himself be?' asked Conley.

'Back,' replied Forsythe. 'Back behind the others.'

'That figures,' said Benton.

But Forsythe, casting an annoyed look at the younger man, shook his head. 'Don't kid yourself,' he said bleakly. 'Plummer's been in

136

more battles than you can shake a stick at. He's a good leader; he thinks like a general of the army. He stays back so's he'll be handy for giving orders. But if it comes to much of a fight, boy, you'll see for sure that Jeb Plummer's no coward.' Forsythe dropped back down upon the ground. His face no longer looked fearful; it looked eager now, and anticipatory. He said to Benton, without looking up at him. 'I got a feelin' before this night is over both you fellers'll have seen more of old Jeb Plummer than you'll want to see.'

'That's enough talk now,' said Tim Conley sharply. 'Not another word until I tell you what to say, Forsythe. And after you've said your piece to Plummer, close your damned trap and keep it closed.'

Forsythe looked hard at Conley saying nothing at all.

'Dallas?'

'Yes, Sheriff.'

'Don't get eager like you did with Reilly. Stay low and roll clear after each shot.'

'I figured to,' said Dallas Benton, reddening a little.

'Now just listen,' said Conley. 'Stay still and listen.' He then left Dallas Benton, walked out a ways straining for sound again, and heard it; that oncoming tinkle of a horseman. He went back beside Dallas and knelt down. To Buck Forsythe he said quietly, 'As soon as that man's close enough I'll nudge you. You call out to him; tell him that I'm Kid Reilly. Then invite him up here to share a bottle with you. After you've said that, Forsythe, drop flat and don't move. Understand?'

Forsythe's answer hung fire a second before he grudgingly nodded, saying only, 'Yeah.'

CHAPTER THIRTEEN

Moments passed full of conflicting emotions for the three waiting men. Tim Conley, close beside his prisoner, listened to each distinct oncoming sound, then, when he could barely make out a shadowy, large silhouette, he pushed his hand-gun into Buck Forsythe's ribs.

Forsythe stiffened slightly, sucked back a big breath and called forward in a guarded way: 'Hey! Over here. It's Buck and the Kid.'

That yonder rider became instantly motionless. Conley watched his head turn the slightest bit. He said without raising his voice, 'It sure took you fellers a long time to get back down here.' Then eased off the reins and permitted his animal to resume its forward way.

Conley raised his gun, tracked the rider with it until the man halted again, this time sitting very erectly in his saddle. 'What the hell,' he called. 'Where are you fellers? Stand up or come over here or something . . .' Those last words were spoken in a rising way, as though this wary outlaw sensed something wrong. 'Buck . . .?'

Forsythe's glistening face swung towards Conley. The sheriff swerved his gun and nodded. Forsythe faced forward again and in a very flat tone he said: 'Duck; it's a trap!'

Conley swung his hand-gun and Forsythe almost bowed into the blow. At the same time a gun exploded ahead. Conley, bending with the strike, twisted above Forsythe's unconscious form to see whether Dallas Benton or the unidentified renegade had fired. He saw and heard the startled snort of a horse, the whipping around of its shape, then the withdrawing throb of its beating hooves. He swore.

Close by and slightly ahead Dallas Benton rolled up onto one knee saying, 'I thought he might try something like that, damn him.' He was referring to Buck Forsythe.

'It's done,' snapped Conley. 'Keep your eyes peeled now, kid.'

There came audibly the swift movement of riders beyond sight out on the desert and Conley, cocking his head to listen, crept up where Dallas Benton lay to say softly, 'They're making a surround. Now remember, boy, roll after each shot.'

Conley could hear them moving beyond vision, some passing swiftly east, some west, of where he and Dallas Benton lay. He had this moment, and only this moment, to reflect on Forsythe's perfidy, and although put in deadly peril by this action of Forsythe's, he thought privately that he could respect Buck Forsythe more for it.

Now there was a stillness too deep for feeling, and Conley measured it in his mind. So far, except for that initial rider's calling-out to Forsythe, he had heard no voices at all. Moreover, thus far there had been only the one gunshot.

Beside him Dallas Benton squirmed. 'What're they doin out there?'

'Scouting us up,' responded Conley in a whisper.

'We could give 'em a round or two.'

'No; let them force the fight. Just lie easy and keep quiet.'

It was not an easy thing to do for youthful Dallas Benton, or Tim Conley either for that matter; just lie there waiting for the bullets that might come any time from any direction. Then a bull-bass cried out to them from due south of where they lay.

'Hey up there—you lawmen?'

Conley, as in this identical position earlier, did not reply. The bull-bass voice seemed undisturbed by this; seemed almost not to expect any answer.

'All right. Suit yourselves, boys. You got Reilly and Forsythe—now we'll get you.' There was a momentary pause before this same voice concluded with: 'Close in on 'em, boys. Can't be more'n a couple of them according to Pete.'

Conley twisted for a look at Forsythe. The prisoner lay exactly as he had fallen from Conley's blow, his hands still bound behind him. Dallas Benton hissed to catch the lawman's attention, and when Conley straightened around Dallas pointed southward. 'Watch that big chaparral clump,' he whispered. Conley watched, saw nothing, but continued to keep this particular patch of desert under surveillance.

Out of the eastern reaches came a searching gunshot. It was not close, nevertheless Dallas winced, squirmed around and strained in that direction. Conley was still observing the chaparral clump. He was beginning to turn away when vague and shifting movement snagged at his attention. He did not wait to sight this creeping man again but fired, rolled, fired again, and rolled again. There came then a wild threshing in the bushes and a man raced back down the night beyond sight but clearly audible.

'You didn't hit him,' husked Dallas Benton, 'but you sure scairt hell out'n him.'

Again the easterly gunman fired. This time he shrewdly bracketed the area. First, with a bullet to the left, then with one to the right, then with a third slug dead centre. Although none of these bullets were close, Conley recognised that in this outlaw they had a worthy opponent.

A figure loomed up beyond Conley, behind him to the west. He did not know this man was there until Dallas Benton's whip-sawed breath warned him of peril. He rolled frantically as two crashing explosions exploded nearly in unison. A bullet kicked up dust where Conley had been. The second shot, made by Benton, evidently went wide because Conley, in his swift movement, also sighted that long-armed, beetling and bulky shape, and recognised in that flashing moment the silhouette of the jailer down in Nacori—Pete Bravo. He shot at Bravo, who, instead of fading out in the night, actually loomed larger and shot back. It was a fierce duel but it did not last long. Tim Conley stopped rolling, took good aim and tugged off another shot. Bravo staggered, then his hand-gun blazed back and Conley had to roll again. But behind him Dallas Benton's weapon was throwing lead from a stationary position. Big Pete Bravo wilted; he turned completely around and sank down upon the ground in a sitting position. He was still dry-firing an empty gun when he toppled over and lay flatly upon his back.

But Bravo's sacrifice had been a noble one, whether he had intended it that way or not, because now Jeb Plummer's bull-bass was shouting orders and the other outlaws were pressing in from all sides.

Conley   re-loaded,   sighted   blurring

movement in the west and threw two fast shots in that direction. Dallas Benton, lying upon his back, was hurriedly pushing fresh loads into his pistol-cylinder. Conley fired over him holding in check those closing forms beyond. Then Dallas was back in the battle and Plummer's men, under this steady and lethal raking, fell back.

Now Conley crawled to where Dallas lay and put his mouth to the younger man's ear. 'Come on,' he croaked, 'we've got to get south—away from here. They'll pattern-fire next—and that'll be the end of us if we're still here.'

He did not wait to see whether or not Dallas was following him, but started crawling swiftly farther down the velvet night.

Plummer's men continued to fire at the periphery where Benton and Tim Conley had been, and as the sheriff had anticipated, they were doing this in such a manner that nothing alive could escape being struck sooner or later.

The lawman and the youth were a long two hundred yards south when the firing dwindled, then stopped altogether. They both drew down in the shelter of a nopal bush and remained motionless. Moments passed, each one of which was a miniature eternity. Then Jeb Plummer's recognisable voice came again, loudly indignant and cursing.

'What's the matter with you simpletons anyway? They aren't here. They got away.'

'Like hell,' cried out a second voice.

'Yonder's one of 'em stretched out dead.'

For a space of seconds Plummer said nothing, then he called in a roughened tone. 'That's Buck, damn you. He's deader'n a mackerel too.' Plummer's voice stiffened, its tone savage now and furious. 'Fan out. Find 'em. Damn you anyway—I want them fellers dead. Quit playin' 'em close to your chests now. They're responsible for Buck here, an' I'll offer a hundred dollars in Mex gold for either one of 'em. Now fan out an' find 'em!'

Conley looked around at Dallas Benton. The youth's face was grey in this meagre light, with dapples of sweat at temple and upperlip. Conley said, 'We couldn't help it, kid. I don't feel exactly sorry about Forsythe and I won't say that I do—but we couldn't help it either, so forget it.'

Benton inclined his head without vigour, mumbling, 'Yeah; you're right, Sheriff. Only it was a helluva way to get it—tied up like that and helpless.'

Conley, having heard something west of them, only half heeded. He twisted in this direction listening. The sound came again, a sharp kind of stamping without the accompaniment of spur rowels. It dawned upon him what this was and hope came. 'Come on,' he said rapidly to Benton, and began crawling rapidly westward.

Benton followed the sheriff without inquiry. They had passed along perhaps half a hundred

144

yards when Conley, out in front, faded out low upon the ground. Dallas instantly followed his example. Conley lay for a long time absolutely motionless. Ahead stood five horses. Four of these animals were saddled and bridled. The fifth beast was rigged out in Mex *alforjas* each *pannier* obviously empty, for as this pack-horse moved nervously along with his companions, the large pack boxes rose and fell in an unmistakably bouncing way which showed they could have nothing in them.

Dallas came up beside the prone lawman, assessed what he saw ahead, then put his face close saying, 'They must think that Sunflower bank holds a heap of gold to bring a pack rig that size.'

Conley nodded saying nothing; he was probing ahead for sign of a guard with the outlaws' horses. He saw none and thought it very probable that Plummer, thinking he had his enemies pinned down well north of this spot, had deployed all his men to the attack.

Conley considered; with a carbine he knew he could stampede Plummer's animals. But he had no carbine so he started closer. Dallas Benton dutifully followed after. They had covered an additional hundred or so feet when Conley halted again, set his elbow deeply into the earth, steadied his gun-hand at the wrist with fingers of his free hand, took aim and fired. The bush where Plummer's horses were tethered shook violently; dust flew from it; its thorny branches whipped wildly striking the tender nostrils of those tied animals, and what both Conley and Dallas Benton anticipated, occurred. The beasts plunged in fierce panic. The bush broke and three of those frightened animals broke away racing with heads and tails high, off into the desert. One animal and the pack-horse did not get free, although both fought their head-ropes desperately, then gradually settled down again, only snorting; standing, stiff-legged with ears nervously sweeping back and forth, blowing outward in diminishing panic.

Conley, hearing the understanding shouts of the returning outlaws, sat up and caught Benton's attention with a hard grip upon the younger man's upper arm.

'Take that horse,' ordered the sheriff, 'and ride for it. Go far out and around—then make a bee-line for Sunflower. Round up a posse and come back as swiftly as you can.'

Benton began to protest. 'Sheriff; you can't hold 'em with odds of three-to-one!'

'Hold 'em hell,' ripped out Conley. 'I don't have to hold 'em. They can't go anywhere in this desert on foot. Now get going.'

Benton might have protested more but Tim Conley swung away from him saying, 'They're running down this way. Move, damn you, Benton—*Move!*'

Dallas Benton moved; he whirled up off the ground and raced for the solitary saddle animal ahead. He was tearing loose the reins and spinning around to rise up and settle across this beast's saddle when, back where he'd left Conley, a savage rattle of gunshots erupted. Dallas listened to this briefly, then did as he'd been ordered; whipped this strange horse around and went plunging westward through the echoing night.

Conley heard him make good his escape while he was raking the northerly approaches to the spot where he lay, with low-holding shots. He was gratified to hear a man's anguished voice cry out, then turn to bleating profanity; he had been struck in the leg and was calling for aid. Conley placed this voice with no difficulty, bracketed it with three rapid shots, and there was no more crying out from that direction, only a low, moaning cursing.

Now came the identifiable voice of Jeb Plummer again, this time raging over the loss of their animals. Conley enjoyed the brigand chieftain's discomfort until, from well west of the lawman, a shrill voice trumpeted into the night that the pack-horse was still tied.

'Get on him,' cried out Plummer now, anxiety making his voice reedy. 'Get on him an' go fetch back them other critters.'

Conley considered these words; evidently Jeb Plummer did not know that one of his foemen had escaped towards Sunflower on one of the horses his crew had ridden up out of Mexico. Conley smiled over this, placed

Plummer's voice and fired in that direction. There came back a high cry, then a blaze of retaliatory gunfire. Conley began to swiftly move away.

CHAPTER FOURTEEN

He got as close to the riderless horse standing where only a short time before there had been four other animals as he dared, and he waited. It was a long wait; clearly the outlaw Plummer had ordered to get on the pack animal was not eager to show himself that high above this night-darkened ground. Conley fretted; around him could distinctly be heard the surreptitious little sounds of men moving in. Still the renegade did not approach that lone, tethered animal. Finally, Conley had to move, behind him were the sounds of two men getting close. He ducked low and scuttled farther southward managing to weave back and forth so that, if others sighted his movements, they would not be able to sight them long because he kept constantly putting bushes behind him.

Somewhere far back a gun went off. Conley paused to look around. This shot, though, had obviously been only to draw him out. He did not return the shot, but scuttled westward now, hurrying, getting up into a crouch when he thought it safe to do so, and running swiftly in an angling way which brought him eventually back around, and above, the spot where he had earlier tied the three livery animals which he and Dallas Benton—and dead Buck Forsythe—had ridden south from Sunflower.

The animals were not there.

He went forward to examine the ground. Even in that steely pale light he could see where one horse had worked constantly to free itself. He drew upright briefly to finger the broken bush. Then he smiled to himself without mirth; the barn-sour horse he'd ridden had been more of a 'home-goer' than he'd thought. He had not only worried himself free of his restraining tether, but had also, by breaking away that one tough limb, freed the other two beasts.

Conley moved away from this spot, finally, when Plummer's bull-bass came distantly to him, directing the outlaws to form skirmish order and sweep forward northward. Evidently, Conley now thought, the renegades had determined that none of their enemies were still southward.

Conley considered that deep voice a moment in thought; Plummer had not ordered this sweep made simply to kill an enemy or two. He had arrived at a rather obvious conclusion, apparently, and was moving now to carry it out.

There was no way for Plummer's gang to get

back over the line into the security of Nacori without horses. Not even an Apache could have crossed that southerly desert in summertime's broad daylight. There was, then, only one alternative left to black-bearded Jeb Plummer; he must hike north several miles, steal horses in Sunflower, then hope he could escape detection long enough to get a good start down-land towards Mexico.

Conley unshipped his revolver, plugged in full loads and knelt in thought behind a slatternly old chaparral bush. Plummer would perhaps be mid-way between Sunflower and where they all were now, by the time Dallas Benton had recruited a posse and started south again. The chances were excellent that Plummer, vastly more experienced than Dallas was, would either anticipate or hear Benton's posse, and slip past it. After that, thought Tim Conley, it would be a matter of time: How long Dallas searched for the outlaws down in the desert, and how swiftly Plummer and his survivors could hoof it to Sunflower. He was confident that once Plummer got mounted again, Dallas Benton would never again get close enough to the bandits to even hear them.

He considered heading back for Sunflower on foot himself; then a much better idea came to him. He was turning it over in his mind, beginning to examine and perfect it, when dead-ahead came the disgruntled voice of trudging men.

'Hey; dammit, slow down will you. Me'n Ace got barked shins. We can't hobble along so fast.'

Conley slunk back westerly, located a denned-under chaparral clump and backed into it awkwardly—and painfully.

'Jeb; this is a waste of time,' someone said plaintively. 'They're plumb gone by now.'

Plummer's voice struck strongly through these whining sounds of unhappy men. 'You'd better hope they didn't make for Sunflower, is all I got to say.'

'We could hunt up one of them ranches north or east o' town,' someone suggested. 'We don't have to walk right into town, do we?'

'It's the closest source of animals,' growled Plummer, then added to it a phrase which made Conley understand how Plummer's thoughts were turning. 'I'd give a thousand dollars in Mex gold to know who engineered that attack and who led it. I'd give five thousand for his head rollin' at my feet, too.'

'That lawman from Sunflower,' groaned a walking man whom Conley could vaguely make out as he hobbled along, badly limping. 'He's a hell-roarer I've heard it said.'

'He didn't roar very loud when we hit that stage,' muttered someone unpleasantly.

Far back now, came a disgruntled voice, saying, 'Where's Reilly an' Cassady? I got a bad feelin' about them two. How come 'em to miss out on this raid, anyway? Especially that cussed Cassady; he's been drinkin' more'n usual lately down in Nacori. I got a bad feelin' about him.'

'Cassady be damned,' swore Jeb Plummer, looming up where Tim Conley could get a good look at him. 'I'm not the least bit concerned about Burl Cassady. What's puzzlin' me is how Buck and the Kid got trapped by that hick-town lawman in Sunflower.'

'Not me,' piped up a reedy voice. 'What I'd like to know is how much chance we got o' getting out o' this mess.'

'We'll get out,' said Plummer reassuringly. 'It's a heap easier to skyline mounted men on a night as dark as this one is, then it is us fellers on foot. You just keep your eyes open and your ears too.'

Conley scarcely breathed; the limping, trudging shadows passed along, some with carried carbines, all with hand-guns riding handily in hip-holsters, in appearance as deadly as roiled rattlers. Only one man was missing—Pete Bravo. The others paced gloomily along beside big Jeb Plummer whose fierce eyes continually raked the countryside round about, and whose bearded face looked darkly evil in that pewter light.

Conley let them get a goodly distance onward before emerging to stand scarcely breathing in their wake. Voices, whiningly plaintive or disgustedly complaining, dimmed out up ahead. Conley waited a time before

152

moving at all, then he went forward in a cautious and leisurely way, trailing after Jeb Plummer's disgruntled outlaw band.

The night was beginning to assume that chill coolness that presaged the small hours. Conley enjoyed it despite his almost drugged weariness. Far off a coyote tongued; moments later another answered. The two of them signalled back and forth for a short while then the desert hush settled down as deeply silent as before. Conley could no longer hear Plummer's men up ahead so he picked up his gait a little, until, dimly audible, the sound of voices came again.

Plummer was picking up speed. He evidently, or so Tim Conley surmised, anticipated the nearness of dawn and wished to do what he must accomplish before daylight caught him.

Conley wondered about Dallas Benton; it seemed that he had been gone a long time, although of this Conley was not certain. Sometimes, when a person was desperately occupied, time seemed to race past; other times it crept with eternal slowness, and now, because Tim Conley rarely carried a pocket-watch, he had no idea what time it actually was.

He skylined the horizon, but there lay only that continuing flow of deep purple in that direction.

He pushed along, slightly faster, until he

again picked up the sound of Jeb Plummer's walking crew. Then instead of hanging well back as he'd been doing, he closed up on them until it was possible to make out the voices clearly.

Someone was complaining of a blistered heel. Another man, evidently one of the wounded, said strongly that he'd rather wait right where he was until his comrades secured horses and came back. To this Jeb Plummer had a curt answer.

'Suppose we're chased?'

That thought dissolved the complaining man's objections. He obviously could visualise his fate if he were by-passed by his friends and apprehended by a posse of angered townsmen. He muttered something profane and kept right on hobbling along.

'Where did them fellers go?' queried one man. 'I didn't hear no horses runnin' past us.'

Again Plummer spoke, evidently able to understand whom this renegade was referring to because he, also, was thinking of their attackers. 'That's been puzzlin' me,' he muttered. 'I didn't hear 'em leave either.'

'Maybe they're still back there. Maybe we clipped 'em an' they crawled into the brush.'

'It's not likely,' rejoined Plummer. 'If one of 'em was the Sunflower lawman—he's got a reputation for not givin' up.'

'Then,' exclaimed the other outlaw, 'they're still behind us somewhere.'

154

Plummer had been considering this, for he now said, 'Y'know; I been wonderin' about that. If they are we might be in a little trouble.'

'Why?'

'You dumb or something?' Plummer demanded of his comrade. 'If they're trailin' us an' makin' no attempt to stop us from gettin' to Sunflower after more horses, then it means they know that on ahead we're going to walk into more trouble.'

This speculation had a sobering effect upon the others. For a while none of them said anything at all, then one man—the man with the reedy voice—spoke up. 'What you reckon we ought to do, Jeb?'

'Exactly what we are doing. We got to have the horses—that's plain enough. The difference is—when we get closer to Sunflower we'll drift into town one at a time. From different directions, you see, and we won't any of us use the main roadway. We'll slip around on both sides o' town, find horses, then drift back out of town, still one at a time.'

'It might work,' a man's considering voice conceded. 'Where'll we meet afterwards?'

'We won't,' said Plummer. 'Just light out for Nacori and make sure each of you get over the line. Afterwards we'll come together again like always at Gomez's *Cantina Libertad*.'

Again the men were silent. Conley heard only the faint music of their spurs for several minutes, then someone said softly, 'We ought to make an ambush, Jeb; if them fellers are behind us maybe we could drygulch 'em and take *their* horses.'

'This close to Sunflower?' said Plummer in a scorning tone. 'The first shot'd have the whole damned town down on us.'

Conley breathed a sigh of relief; it had occurred to him that this notion might appeal to Plummer, and while he was forewarned and therefore reasonably secure from this stated peril, it did not at all dovetail with his ideas.

He was jerked away from his private thoughts by one of those distant shapes stopping. Conley grew instantly still. Plummer called back to this man: 'What the hell are you doin'?'

'Cuttin' myself a stick,' the halted man explained, worrying with his Barlow knife at a tough chaparral bush. 'That danged bullet crease in my leg's hurtin' something fierce.'

Plummer said no more; he and his companions milled grumpily as the wounded man completed his endeavours, then they all started forward again, Conley too.

CHAPTER FIFTEEN

A short while later on a mounted man came jogging audibly southward. They all heard him, even Conley, whose heart turned over; he doubted that Dallas Benton would be riding alone and yet, because Dallas was young and inexperienced he was not positive about this. Up ahead Jeb Plummer gave a sharp order. His ragged crew faded out in the darkness. There settled now a great depth of stillness. It was ultimately broken by a soft voice calling outward.

'Oh, Jeb. Jeb; you out there? Hey, Jeb.'

Plummer said something loud enough for Conley to hear him indistinguishably, then his voice came on stronger. 'Over here, Cal. Where are the damned horses?'

'Not a sign of 'em,' said the rider, jogging into sight on the pack-animal.

Plummer cursed again, then said, 'Any other sign?'

To this the dismounting horseman made no audible reply but Conley, close enough to see these two men, saw him wag his head negatively.

'All right,' growled Plummer, black beard and fierce eyes briefly touched by the arcing light of a falling star so that even Conley, well southward, could see his clear countenance. 'Come on, fellers; it's only a little way onward now.'

Conley watched the outlaw chieftain tilt his head and gaze at the sky. As his men began moving out again Plummer said, 'It's goin' to be close, boys. Dawn isn't far off.'

This observation did more to speed up the

157

dawdling steps of his men than anything else Plummer could have said to them would have done. Conley now had to lengthen his own stride to keep up.

The riderless pack-animal was being led along. Conley kept his eyes on this hulking silhouette; was considering it with particular attention because he knew, if another fight started, someone would try to escape on it, when a man walking slightly ahead of Jeb Plummer went stiff in mid-stride saying swiftly: 'Listen; riders coming!'

Conley also heard them. Clearly, the horsemen were passing along without any attempt at silence. Also, just as clearly, they were coming from the direction of Sunflower.

Someone up ahead breathed a faint curse, then said, 'It's a posse. I'll bet you a good savinna horse it's a damned posse from Sunflower. Jeb; them fellers *did* pull out and head back for more men.'

'Shut up,' snapped Plummer, standing fully erect and plainly in Conley's sight, his slightly moving head picking up the sound of those oncoming riders, tracing out their route and numbers with no great effort. Then Plummer spun towards his men. 'Take cover,' he said quickly, 'and not a sound. Don't make a sound of any kind—at all. *Move!*'

Conley, watching the renegades dim out into the dry and crackling chaparral, was interested to see how swiftly and competently

158

the outlaw crew disappeared. He, also, went low upon the ground.

Ahead, close enough now for Conley to hear their smallest sounds—the abrasive rub of *rosaderos*, the tinkle of chain and rowels, even the good fragrance of cigarettes—came the band of bunched-up horsemen. Conley rose up a little as they were silhouetted, counting them and seeking Dallas Benton. He sighted Dallas first; he was well ahead of the others, riding warily with a carbine balancing across his lap. Behind him were twelve other mounted men. What made it initially appear to Conley that there were more than twelve riders was the fact that one man, near the end of the posse, was leading a saddled but riderless horse.

Dallas was doing exactly what Jeb Plummer had anticipated, he was riding with his head cocked for sounds. He was also, as Tim Conley saw, angling in such a fashion that he would pass along the westerly side of the spot where Plummer's men had gone to earth and were now lying like stones, scarcely breathing. Dallas's posse would pass on within moments and now, Conley knew, was the time for him to make the move he had earlier considered.

He could have called out, of course, but Jeb Plummer would have instantly known discovery was imminent and would have ordered a fusillade fired southward towards Conley's voice. Conley therefore rummaged

159

his pockets for matches, crawled from dry bush to dry bush setting little fires. In a surprisingly brief time these summer-dry chaparral bushes were fiercely burning. Conley continued to move, speedily now, pantingly, making a large surround of the area where Plummer and his band lay hiding, until he had a fiercely illuminating fire burning completely around Plummer's crew. He then called to Dallas, got back an answer, and trotted forward where the possemen were drawing away from the heat, coming together with their wary faces and their ready guns, converging upon Dallas, as suspicious and wary of this abrupt blazing as was Dallas Benton himself.

Conley gave Benton no chance to say a word. He was breathing hard from his recent exertion, so flagged eastward towards the surrounding blaze with one upflung arm.

'They're inside that fire-circle. Every one of them.'

An older man at Benson's side, his face screwed down against the brightness and the increasing heat, said, 'Hell; they can't stand that for long.'

Another posse rider, inching closer, said, 'It'll be like shootin' crows on a roost.'

To this man, and the others, Conley raised his voice. 'No shooting. They'll be blinded and won't be able to see us out here, even if they want to fight. Get down off your horses and stay back. It won't take Jeb Plummer long to figure out he's beaten.'

The possemen, including Dallas Benson, did as Conley ordered; retreated beyond pistol range and waited. Conley accepted the canteen a shadowy rider held forth, drank from it, returned it and said to Dallas Benton, 'Come on; you'n I've put up with a lot from Plummer. We deserve the privilege of bein' up there when he quits.'

The two of them went carefully forward. By now the flames were spreading, leaping horse-high in the paling light of a new day, burning with a crackling, grease-wood-fed intensity. Conley stopped when a staggering man, one arm over his face and a pistol in his upraised hand, broke through the fire nearby to nearly run into them. He caught the man roughly, knocked away the pistol and spun him towards Dallas. The younger man's pistol hit this man hard in the middle. The outlaw gasped, dropped his arm and squinted hard at Dallas's face.

Over the plunging flames and their increasing noise came the voice Tim Conley had anticipated. It was raised in frantic desperation. At Conley's side Dallas said, 'Jeb Plummer,' and Conley nodded.

'Hey out there—we quit. Don't shoot. You hear me—don't shoot we're comin' through.'

Conley said to Dallas: 'Get down. I don't trust him.'

It proved, however, to be an unnecessary

precaution for when Jeb Plummer came racing across the flames he was patting furiously at his great beard, which was singed; he did not even have a gun in his holster. At sight of Tim Conley's upraised gun, steadily tracking him, Plummer threw both arms up high crying: 'Don't shoot; we're through.' He was badly winded from his run, as were the men with him.

'Call up your posse,' Conley said to Dallas, and began to get upright. Dallas hurried back motioning at the waiting possemen. To Jeb Plummer Conley said: 'I think you've been over-rated, Plummer. I'd always heard you were a regular cougar of a man.'

Plummer stood there, several inches taller than Tim Conley, his fiercely bearded lips sucked back, staring at the sheriff. He finally spoke, scarcely moving his mouth at all. 'I'm not complaining,' he said looking fully into Conley's eyes. 'Somewhere is a man who is another man's nemesis. You've been mine. I fell for your fire-circle like a green kid.'

Conley holstered his weapon. Looking now upon this notorious renegade chieftain, this man of wiles and iron and ruthlessness, he saw something that he respected: Whatever else Jeb Plummer was—he was not a coward.

Conley said to him: 'No; not like a green kid, Plummer. You only been in Texas by all accounts about six or seven years. You came from the middle-border states.'

162

'What's that got to do with it?'

'A lot,' Conley said succinctly. 'You grew up where civilisation is and has been for generations. In Texas, those of us who've come to manhood here learnt tricks most folks never even heard of. That night-trapping with flames is an old Comanche Indian trick. A Texas outlaw wouldn't have fallen for it.'

'I see,' said Plummer, turning a little look over the crowd of grim faces coming towards him behind Dallas Benton. He studied these silent, grim possemen only a moment then turned contemptuously away from them, fastening his piercing gaze again upon Tim Conley. 'Tell me something, Sheriff; were you down in Nacori?'

'I was.'

'And you got Burl Cassady, didn't you?'

'I did. He's in my jail at Sunflower right now.'

Behind Conley Dallas Benton cleared his throat and shuffled his feet. The men around him looked quickly in his direction. Dallas avoided their looks and studied his boot toes with solemn concentration. Conley saw none of this; he was still gazing upon his prisoner and the bedraggled, sullen men with him.

'Another thing,' said Conley. 'Kid Reilly is dead and your own shots killed Forsythe.'

'Reilly?' said Plummer, then shrugged. 'You trick him too?'

'Not exactly,' said Conley turning towards

Dallas Benton. 'Let's get riding, boy, it's breaking day.'

They mounted, all but their prisoners, and started slowly towards Sunflower. Out of the east's farthest curving came the summer sun, popped up over the horizon like a seed popped from a grape. Jeb Plummer's men trudged along looking daggers at the mounted possemen, but Plummer himself, his face unreadable behind his beard, did not look back at all; he swung along at a long pace all the way into town. Even there where humiliation could not have helped but touch him, he looked neither right nor left as townsmen gathered murmuring his name, pointing and cat-calling, but walked sturdily as far as the jailhouse with his head up and his piercing dark gaze cowing all who met this hawk-like stare. There he stopped, leaned upon the jailhouse wall and waited for Conley to dismount and walk forward. Then Plummer led his men into the jailhouse, stopped in the middle of the room and faced around.

Conley tossed aside his hat, went to his desk and picked up the cell-keys; he was straightening up with these in his fist when he froze, staring past Jeb Plummer.

Burl Cassady's cell was empty!

A frightening thought struck Conley hard, making him wince. 'Dallas,' he called out. 'Dallas—come in here.'

Benton appeared. Behind him men crowded

164

into the office partially filling the office, completely blocking the door and standing outside peering over shoulders.

'Dallas; where is Cassady?'

'I meant to tell you, Sheriff. I started to tell you on the ride in, but—'

'Where is he?'

'Dead, Sheriff.'

Conley turned completely around to face the younger man. He said nothing but his stare fairly shouted the question.

'He hung himself, Sheriff.'

'What!'

'That's the gospel truth,' a townsman said, speaking up loudly from behind Dallas Benton. 'Some fellers heard he was in here an'—well—they come down to look at him, an' by golly—'

'Yes,' snapped Conley in a clipped and angry tone. 'I can imagine. They just wanted to look at Cassady—but they happened to have lariats in their hands.' Sheriff Tim paused, reading faces. 'A lousy lynch-mob.'

No one said a word. Scarcely an eye met the sheriff's bitter stare. He stood stiffly quiet for a long time, then he said, 'Which one of you had a hand in it?'

'That's the honest truth, Sheriff,' said a man from far back. 'No one lynched him. Maybe the mob scairt him that bad—but I give you my word, when the fellers come back with a saw to cut him out o' the cell—there he hung. Dead by his own hand.'

Conley gazed at Dallas. 'Did you cut him down?' Dallas nodded. 'He was dead when you got back here?' Another nod. Tim Conley lifted the hand holding those cell-keys. 'Lock these other ones up,' he said to young Benton, then made an angry motion at the possemen and townsmen. 'Clear out,' he commanded. 'Go on home and sit down to breakfast, boys— and think about what a fine, courageous thing you did last night. Go on; get out of here!'

The men passed almost silently out into the freshening daylight and Conley slammed the door behind them. When he faced around Jeb Plummer was smiling at him. He said: 'Don't take it so hard, Sheriff. Cassady wouldn't have been around much longer anyway. He was startin' to drink too much an' he was gettin' reckless. Reckless fellers don't last long when they ride with me.' Plummer yawned, felt his singed beard, and said almost cheerfully, 'How about some breakfast?'

Conley, a thought suddenly striking him, said to Dallas Benton, 'Get them some food. I'll be back after a while.'

Dallas Benton scowled after the sheriff's retreating figure but said nothing.

Conley hastened to the Hardin place, was raising his fist to strike the door when it opened slowly inward and Rose Bell met his troubled, haggard look with a glance as serenely peaceful and untroubled as a woman's glance could be. Conley stood there with his fist still raised.

Rose Bell made a very faint smile. 'Are you going to strike me, or come inside?'

Conley dropped his hand, swept off his hat and moved into the cool, quiet interior of the Hardin house. 'How is Elizabeth?' he asked. 'Dallas told me the liveryman said—'

'She is doing very well. The haemorrhage has stopped and she's beginning to eat again.' Rose Bell let her eyes move slowly down Tim Conley and back up again to his face. 'Sheriff,' she said, half-humourously, 'you're a sight.'

Conley didn't smile back at her. 'Cassady is dead, ma'm.'

'Yes; I know.'

'Well . . .'

'You don't have to say anything, Sheriff. I heard about it this morning quite early.'

'And?' prompted Conley softly.

She met his gaze steadily. 'I know I should say I'm sorry, Sheriff. I should feel sad too but I'm not a hypocrite. I'm not sorry.' Her gaze became slightly clouded and she concluded in a little voice by saying, 'Do you think I am a terrible person? I think I am.'

Conley let his breath out slowly. He replaced his hat saying gravely to her, 'You would know better than I whether you should feel differently about this. I just wanted to be sure to know that I had no hand in it.'

'I know you didn't, Tim. And I'm glad you

167

'weren't here when it happened, too.'

'Well . . .' said Conley lamely. 'I guess I ought to go shave and get cleaned up.'

Her cool gaze turned amused. 'Sheriff,' she said. 'Did you think I'd be gone from Sunflower?'

'As a matter of fact I did kind of have an idea like that. That's partly why I came over here as soon as we got back. Otherwise I'd have cleaned up first.'

'Would it have made any difference to you if I had moved on?'

Conley answered honestly: 'It would have made a big difference, Rose Bell. You might say it was thinking of you that kept me coming over that cussed desert.'

Rose Bell's gaze swept fully upwards, there was no longer any amusement in it. 'Go home,' she told him quietly holding his eyes with hers. 'Have a bath and sleep all day. Then, after nightfall if you still think it's important to you that I'm still here, come back.'

'You'll be here?'

'Tim; I'll be waiting out on the porch.'

Conley's face lost the last of its tightness. He smiled down at her. 'You be here,' he said. 'Hear? I'll be back and we'll have supper at the hotel.'

He reached down to close the door; so did she and their fingers met on the latch. Rose Bell did not at once move her hand.

She said: 'I'll be here, Tim. I've been out

here in the moonlight ever since you rode south.' She made a little smile at him. 'Did you ever pray to a star?'

'No, ma'm, I never did.'

Her voice went deeper, turned soft and warm towards him. 'It works, Tim. Take it from me, it works.'

He did not move so she put up a hand, lay it gently upon his chest and gently pushed. 'You'd better go now.'

He nodded, longing in his eyes like a banner.

Rose Bell watched him pace out to the roadway and turn south. There was a spring in his step. She wondered how a man who had been through all that he had survived could still walk jauntily. She very slowly passed back into the house troubled in thought and spirit. Went along to Elizabeth's room and there sat down oblivious of Elizabeth's close scrutiny.

'Rose Bell; wasn't that Sheriff Tim's voice I heard outside just now?'

'Yes.'

'Why didn't he come in?'

'He just got back from Nacori.'

'Was Dallas with him?'

'No, not with him at the door, but he rode back with him.'

Elizabeth's steady regard turned solemn. 'Rose Bell?'

'Yes.'

'It won't help to grieve.'

Rose Bell looked up; understanding came slowly to shadow her face. She said soberly, 'I'm not grieving, Elizabeth. Not the way you think. There's not a tear left in me to shed over Burl Cassady.'

'Then what is it? You're unusually serious.'

'It's Tim Conley. He . . . well; he's going to take me to supper tonight at the hotel and I think I know what he's going to say.' Rose Bell's midnight-eyes were very dark, like pools of liquid lava. 'I don't know how to answer him, Elizabeth.'

'Say "yes". There never was a finer man than Sheriff Tim. He'll make you happy.'

'I never doubted that, Elizabeth. What's troubling me is—will I be able to make him happy?' Rose Bell stirred on the chair. 'My life has been nothing I'm proud of; he deserves better than he's likely to get.'

Elizabeth's face turned sweet, turned gentle. She said to Rose Bell, 'When I was a little girl Tim told me several times not to judge people by what lay in their pasts. To only value them according to what they do with that part of their lives that remains to them. When I was little I didn't understand exactly what he meant but I always remembered the words because he never told me anything that wasn't true.

'Of course, within the last few years I came to know what he meant by that, Rose Bell, but until tonight—until right this minute—I never really understood it completely. May I ask you a personal question?'

Rose Bell nodded, saying nothing.

'Do you want to make him happy starting now?'

'Very much, Elizabeth. I want that very much.'

'Then say "yes" when he asks you to marry him, and remember what he told me when I was a little girl. That it's not what's past that counts; it's what lies ahead of you and what you do with it.'

Rose Bell smiled through a gathering mist, crossed over to sit upon the side of Elizabeth's bed, and quite spontaneously they came together, neither of them being able any longer to hold back the tears.